Delphine and The Dangerous Arrangement

by Alicia Cameron

Dedication

To Alan, my very best friend, unpaid personal assistant (!) and love. Quite fond.

FREE!!!

A short novella, FREE just for you:

The Marquise de Chabernet, her French grandmother, had fixed her with glittering eyes and told her when she was but ten years old, 'If there is something that you want in this life, *mon ange*, do not believe *anyone* who says you cannot have it.'

http://bit.ly/2vXZLhh

CHAPTER 1

Considering that the house had received no visitors for some years, excepting the occasional visits by old Mr Rigby-Blythe, and considering that she had just become an orphan, Delphine Delocroix's house seemed remarkably full of relatives. Especially aunts. There were probably a similar number of uncles, but as they gathered around sipping wine and indulging in desultory conversation, the worst she could say of them is that they blocked any heat from the cavernous fireplace. The aunts on the other hand gathered around one like gnats, even entering her bedchamber and pulling and picking at her dress and hair, buzzing with words that overlapped each other so much that she barely understood them. They were her mother's sisters, which did not recommend them to Delphine, but as unlike her in appearance as they were each other. Her mother had brown hair, one aunt was fair beneath the turban, another dark and definite. The third was plump, unlike the others, and her hair was russet as an autumn day.

The throng followed her downstairs, surrounding her, and flew around her whilst she entered the drawing room which contained sundry male relatives that she had been briefly introduced to, as well as a number of unknown neighbours that the aunts had seen fit to invite to the funeral. These last could be seen to have wandering eyes, taking in the rooms and the appointments of furniture of the biggest house in the vicinity, about which their curiosity had been denied so long. She too, they had taken in hungrily - the young lady they had been permitted to bow to, never approach, as she sat stiffly upright in the carriage whilst her mother entered one of the village draper shops.

She was twenty-two years old and alone in the world, despite the chattering hoard that she had only just met. Mr Rigby-Blythe was her only acquaintance, and she met his ancient eye as she entered. She suspected he was to blame for the swarm. He was wearing the same rusty black suit as he always wore, and was so similarly ruined and rusty in his person that he always gave alarm, lest he gave his last breath under one's anticipatory eye. Only his watery eyes gave any sign of life. They glittered at her as they had in those few minutes that she had been allowed to sit with him - before his lawyerly business with her mama.

There was to be a will reading, of course. Delacroix House was a large manor that had been raised in old Queen Anne's day and her mother had been proud of it. Its many features had been spelt out to her, as had the life story of the great-great grandfather who had built it. She was aware that she came from a long illustrious line, whose closeness to monarchs had resulted in being granted many favours, including a Baronetcy that was now lost for lack of a male heir. It was a knife in her father's heart, her mother had frequently informed her, that she had been born female, so much so that he had not been able to look at her. His death three years after she had been born had made this less of a blow than it may have been. She did not remember him. But the frequency of her mother's reminder let her know that the knife had also penetrated the second parental heart. But then, so much that she had done in her young life had wounded her mother. 'You will oblige me, Delphine, by …' Refraining from slouching. Modulating your tone. Foregoing to run. Keeping your opinions to yourself. Eating what has been provided for you. Straightening your dress. Avoiding speaking to the servants. Wearing what I set for you. Reading what I choose for you. Never entering my chamber.

She was wearing a dress her mama had had made for her for this very day, once she knew that consumption was hastening her demise. It was of the finest black silk brocade, over an under-dress of heavy black satin. The whole thing had about twice as much skirt as any lady's present, they wearing the finest muslin or silk, caught under the bust, with skirts that draped to show the body. Aunt Eloise, in particular, though a woman of fifty-five, wore a dress that was so diaphanous as to be shocking. On her fair head was a silken turban and a plume (dyed black, of course) and though she had fretted at Delphine's dress, Delphine considered her deranged. Her own gown must have cost a great deal more than her aunt's feather-weight affair. And that lady must be pierced with cold in these ancient, but draughty, halls.

Delphine made her stately way around the room, nodding to the village people, which was more condescension than she would have been allowed to show in her mother's presence. A poor little scrap of a woman in a fluttery grey dress moved forward and put out her hand saying, 'Oh my dear, how very sorry-'

Delphine stopped and looked at the hand. She had no notion what to do with it, no one had had the temerity to offer her such intimacy in her life. One of the aunts, plump good natured Aunt Sybilla, said, 'Oh, Miss Beauford, so kind of you to have come,' and shook the poor lady's hand lightly.

Miss Beauford's eyes looked into Delphine's with an expression she had never seen before, but that she feared maybe pity, and then smiled faintly and fluttered away.

That such a woman should pity her held Delphine stiff with humiliation. But she was moved to say to her aunt, 'Beauford … but that is Mama's own name?'

'Of course my dear, Beauford is my late Papa's name. We were all Miss Beaufords. Phoebe Beauford is, I believe, a second or third cousin of yours. Surely you were made aware when your mother introduced you?'

'I have never been introduced to her before.'

Aunt Sybilla stared. 'But she is a relative. She lives in the *village*.' Delphine said nothing. 'Perhaps your mama feared that she and her sister would batten onto their more prosperous relatives.' She looked again at Delphine's face. 'But it is very strange of Emilia not to apprise you of-'

Her aunt led the way forward to another group of villagers, none of whom repeated the attempt at intimacy, but contented themselves with slight bows (the gentlemen) or curtsies (the ladies) which Delphine reprised, even more slightly.

#

Lady Marguerite Pelleter, the most brisk of the aunts, with thick dark brows as decided as her character, and a chanteuse dress draped *à la Diane*, was regarding Delphine from a distance. 'She holds herself very high. She's as cold as Emilia.'

'I think, don't you, that we should give her a chance,' said Lady Eloise Carswell, she of the shocking gown, but with large blue eyes that expressed her caring nature, 'She has had only one pattern-card for behaviour and I do not wish to speak ill of the dead, but Emilia was-'

'Yes. We all must do what we can for her. But if she really is of Emilia's nature-'

'Quite!'

#

After the guests had left and the will had been read, there had been the chattering dinner to be endured before Delphine had been released to her bedchamber. She was in shock. As well as the trial of the whole day, exposed to more society than in her whole life preceding, she had just found out that she was very wealthy indeed.

She had previously considered that her mother's choice of restricted society and travel stemmed from a similarly restricted income. They ate frugally and had a fire in very few of the rooms. Their clothes were the only luxury mama had permitted - this Delphine had thought of as display of consequence for the village and the servants - with all the other economies practised to support the display. So much she had worked out. But it was quite untrue. The Delacroix estate was the largest and wealthiest in the county. Her late father had owned other properties throughout England, some let to wealthy families, including a whole London Square. There were bonds and investments of many kinds, and apparently she could ransom a king.

Her maid Susan, over forty with a face of frozen biliousness, had that night removed her mistress's clothes silently, but permitted herself a few acid words before she left the bedchamber.

'Your wealth will attract only the sewer rats of London to your side - Lady Delacroix said as much to me before her death.' The bitter lines around her mouth tightened before she turned to go. She had been her mother's devoted slave - and spy.

Delphine seldom exchanged words with this attendant of all her young days. 'You need not worry about London, Susan.'

‘You do not go, then?’ said that upright dame, surprised - and pleased, the girl thought.

‘Oh yes,’ said Delphine, ‘at the beginning of the season. But you will not accompany me.’

Susan blinked, then left her with a look that could turn milk.

Wealth, had thought Delphine, was already having some benefits.

#

'The richest?'

'Oozing'

'How wonderfully vulgar you are, Hildegard. How came town to be ignorant of this? If we cannot trust the wag tongues, what use have they?'

'Lived with her mother in the country. Religious women.'

'As are we all. Young, then?'

'Practically past her prime. Twenty-two, I believe.’

'Youth gone and the bloom left her cheek. But life teaches us that there are always trials to be borne.'

'Old Midas says she is richer even than him.'

'Then I suppose we must forgive her the face.'

'Her face?'

'The face that prevented the rich mama from presenting her to the town.'

'Foggy saw her. No disfigurement that he could see. Just dresses in an old out-dated manner - oddly, he said.'

'Well, Foggy himself dresses oddly so we'll give little credence to that... I do hope it doesn't start a new fashion. Just when society has settled to a dream of classicism - it would be bad manners for a rich young *debutante* to attempt a coup. I should have to cut my hair. But a wondrously rich orphan with no obvious disfigurement. It's a rare, unprotected, prize.'

'As to that, there are a number of maternal aunts.'

Gascoigne sighed. 'It is ever thus. Who?'

'Well, Lady Carswell, Foggy's mother, of course, Mrs Lynfield, and Lady Mags Pelleter.'

'Good God! As well take on the Duke.'

'Wellington might be preferable to Lady Mags. Well, anyway, I believe I will try my luck at the Castlereigh's ball where it is rumoured she will make her first appearance!'

'So, I suppose, must I. The hounds are even now baying at my door. How desperately dull. Should I wear a wig, do you think, to curry favour?'

'Yes. It sounds odd - hair a mile high like portraits of one's grandmamma, Foggy says.'

#

Delphine Delacroix was sitting on her Aunt Sybilla's pale gold covered settee which matched another three such (plus several chairs) in her aunt's commodious morning room in Russell Square. Mrs Sybilla Lynfield was the richest of her sisters, having failed, happily, to catch a poor aristocrat like the others. Mr Lynfield was handsome rich and kind, delighting in his plump and amusing little woman. Fifty now, her French embroidered muslin dress was in a rich green colour that cleverly complimented the red in her hair. This was styled in the latest (and daring) short crop, enhanced today by a broad green silk band.

Her niece was wearing a heavily corseted blue brocade dress, which may make some suitable upholstery for any number of chairs, and her brown hair (despite the strict instructions given by her hostess to her lady's maid) was piled on her head precariously in coils and rolls (no doubt some of them false) with an ornate pleated ribbon arrangement threaded though. One ringlet hung over her shoulder to finish it. It was surprising that she did not also wear powder and patch. She sat perfectly straight in her chair and did not move. Her face had regular features, was triangular in shape; her large turquoise eyes could have offered it distinction, but as their expression was as closed off and cold as her mother's, they failed to do so.

Here sat the richest unmarried girl in England, thought Mrs Lynfield, and much good has it done her.

It had been thought by the three aunts that Sybilla, not having a daughter to bring out, would be the person best suited to take Delphine in charge after the strict period of mourning had passed. They had all determined to rescue her from Delacroix House, where she had lived as a bird in a gilded cage all her life, speaking only to her mother and to servants, allowed no visitors. Mrs Lynfield herself had, five years ago, written to her sister offering to bring the girl out - but she had received no reply.

Mrs Sybilla Lynfield had been chosen to house the girl, since it was obvious that her sisters' as yet unmarried daughters (Christiana Carswell and Lady Roberta Pelleter, both thankfully pretty) would get stampeded underfoot in the attempt to get near Miss Delacroix's fortune. Mrs Lynfield, with only a son away at sea, had happily agreed.

Mr Lynfield (with a change from his usual suave tone) had, last evening, grasped Delphine's shoulders, which caused her to stiffen, and said, 'you are very welcome here, my dear girl.' He'd leaned forward and kissed the girl's cheek, which had caused her eyes to enlarge in shock, as though she had been struck.

When Lord Peregrine (Pinky to his friends), also there with the family to welcome her, had tried his inarticulate best to express his feelings on the occasion, she had almost jumped. Mind you, the big, bluff, face of his lordship coming towards one was a trial, but he meant well. As different as could be to Mr Lynfield's debonair person, he was bluff and a little overweight and heavily dependent on his charming wife. Eloise, the kindest of the sisters, had become engaged to the tortured young man in her first season precisely because he was always strangled with embarrassment when asked to speak to young ladies. Her compassionate heart had sought to make him more comfortable, and eventually he proposed, with Eloise filling in a great many blanks in his declaration with imagination, and she had consented. Lord Carswell, last evening, had made do with patting his niece's arm, which had caused the girl to look at him as if he were an escaped lunatic. Which was unfair, thought Sybilla, he was only an idiot.

It had seemed that all that would be needed to launch her niece on the world was to take her to the best dressmaker in town and update her antiquated (if expensive) wardrobe, have her hair done, and steer her past the shoals of fortune hunters towards some worthy match.

But her niece had proved more difficult than she had imagined. To all her expositions of the latest modern fashions she had asked 'Must I?' and when her aunt had said peevishly that she thought it would be a treat for her, said firmly, 'It is not.'

'Well, it would be a treat for me!' said her exasperated aunt. 'You really cannot be seen in London looking such a fright.'

There was a flicker in Delphine's eye at this, and her soft-hearted aunt was stricken with guilt. 'I did not mean you, but only your clothes.'

'My mama had this fabric imported from Italy at great expense, and had it made in the village by a seamstress who once worked in the finest London establishments.' She heard her aunt mutter, 'Thirty years ago!' but ignored it. 'I must suppose that the cost of my gown is vastly superior to yours.'

'Very likely,' said Sybilla Lynfield, acidly, 'and if you were a cushion, or a dining chair, or some such thing, I would consider you very elegantly appointed. But as you are a young lady making her debut in the polite world, you will wear something fitting.'

The two sets of eyes met each other and Delphine's cool turquoise ones were rather surprised at the fire in her erstwhile kind aunt's. The eyes held for perhaps a minute, then Delphine rose calmly. 'I shall consider the matter,' she said regally and moved from the room.

Her aunt sat with a phoph! on a well upholstered chair and looked at the tall, ancient figure of her butler, who allowed himself to meet her eye briefly. 'I do not know what to do with that girl, Fiennes!' she confided, beyond convention.

'A great deal of spirit,' the butler muttered, with a cough.

'Is that what it is called? More like Emilia's-' she said referencing her dead sister, but she recalled herself. Fiennes knew all her sisters, having worked for her father before her, but it was unbecoming to discuss such things with him. Their eyes met and she did not have to finish with "stubbornness" for him to understand it.

#

Mr Rigby-Blythe had the veiled young lady ushered into his office, reflecting that the discretion of the veils was quite redundant since the dress of the last age (this time a voluminous cloak of purple velvet over a such a profusion of lavender silk as would fashion evening gowns for three young ladies of today) made it quite unnecessary to await the lifting of the veil, to say:

'Miss Delacroix, a pleasure.'

'Mr Rigby-Blythe. We may converse at last.'

Seeing her to the seat beside his large mahogany desk, his eyes twinkled.

'Our stolen conversations at Delacroix House seemed almost clandestine, had I not been an old man.'

Delphine smiled, the first he had seen from her, 'I believe if you had offered for me sir, I may have run away with you.'

'Alas that I had not a steed with the stamina to speed us to Gretna Green!' he smiled.

'No, I believe your Trusty might have failed us before Speltham.' She said, a trifle sadly, mentioning the town twenty miles distance from her home.

'Well, we must not repine for what might have been, my dear girl. What may I do for you? Your uncle Lynfield has said to me quite clearly that I must deal with him in all matters relating to you.'

Delphine frowned. 'And you replied?'

'I did the lawyerly thing my dear, and smiled. If Mr Lynfield chose to conclude that I agreed, he was quite free to do so.'

'I knew, sir, that to further my acquaintance with you would be a joy for me. Now that we are at our leisure to talk, let me enjoy it - might I have some tea?'

With a large gesture of acquiescence, Mr Rigby-Blythe rang a bell.

Over tea Delphine learnt a great many things about her fortune. It would become hers fully when she was twenty-five, although the assumption was that she would have a husband to manage it before then. Her maternal uncle, Mr St John Beauford, now living in Paris, was the executor, with the practical aid, in London, of Mr Rigby-Blythe. All accounts would be sent to Mr Beauford - but he had already resolved on a princely sum as her quarterly pin money. He would be resistant, as any gentleman would, to his niece's interest in the financial matters regarding her estate, for women's brains were not formed to deal with such things.

'I may have other expenses over and above the clothes that my aunts wish to foist on me. Might I draw on you?'

Mr Rigby-Blythe's merry, rheumy old eyes looked into hers, 'I suspect,' he said, 'that you will be a very fashionable and expensive young lady.'

'I do not think so.'

'If there are a plethora of expenses,' he suggested sagely, 'some more than might be considered usual, who knows what bills might be lost among?'

'So I must embrace the dress maker?'

'Oh, I thinks so. And the manteaux-maker and the milliner. And you may wish to set up your stable, perhaps. A number of fashionable young ladies have horses and carriages of the latest design, to tool around the park and be remarked upon.'

'I do not wish to be remarked upon,' said Delphine flatly.

Mr Rigby-Blythe sipped his tea. 'Then you had better not wear the clothes your mother had made for you. They may be finely wrought, but they are so outmoded as to make you a figure of fun.'

Delphine had already been pointed out by people on the street enough to know this to be true. Her resistance to her aunt's entreaties burst like a bubble. She had refused merely to escape another version of her mother's control. But when her true ally told her the same thing, she gave in. At least this way she would no longer be an oddity. 'And the horses?' she enquired.

'Are the sort of expense that your uncle St John would not take issue with. He wishes you to make your mark upon the world so that you may gain a husband and relieve him of the burden of your financial empire. It is rather more than he bargained for at his time of life.'

'Shall you tutor me in the business of my holdings?'

His eyes considered. 'It is perhaps a little tedious work for a young lady, but if you wish it, I will.' He sighed, 'My dear girl, if I might be permitted to call you so, it will do you little good. Your wealth will be dealt with by your husband, whose name we will find out by the end of the season, I have no doubt.'

As if she had not heard him, she said coolly, 'My aunt visits with her sisters on a Thursday afternoon, saving more pressing invitations. They like to speak of me, so it will be quite convenient for me to come to your office on these days, on the pretext of attending the lending library.'

'I should not have guessed that subterfuge would come so easily to you, my dear.'

'I did not previously have the scope.' She saw Mr Rigby-Blythe's eyes water a trifle more than their rheumy best even as he smiled at her jest, and added gently, 'My aunts are a great deal kinder than my mother, sir, in their individual ways. But I fear finding myself in a trap worse than I have lived. Marriage is their answer to all, but I think them all too silly to be trusted with my future.'

'I would I could advise you, my dear, but the polite world is not my area of expertise. I have a few clients, I hear gossip, but I doubt it enough to avoid a possible *mésalliance*.'

'Ah! You do understand. I always believed that you would. Though we exchanged so few words, I saw a wealth of understanding in your eyes.'

'And I in yours. Your mother was a challenging woman. I cannot imagine the life you lived there.'

Delphine's eyes became a little cold. 'She did not like me, but she could never let me become attached to another person. More than one servant was cast off simply for showing me a morsel of affection, including my old nurse. I should like you to find her, sir, and to make sure she was adequately pensioned.'

The lawyer took up his quill and asked some questions, writing down his client's scant knowledge. 'I shall set enquiries in motion at once, it may be that her direction is in some old papers of your mother's that I have not yet perused.'

'Before I left, I visited with Miss Beauford, a cousin of some distance, I understand. She was most thankful that her late sister and she were permitted to live in the cottage by my so-generous parent. Aunt Eloise took me on a polite visit before we left Delacroix, and I could see that even she was shocked. The running water on the wall, the leaking roof and this sweet creature with her mother's china and her clean white linen. How could my mother allow it? No wonder she did not take me to visit my only relative in the village. I wish that her cottage be repaired as quickly as possible.'

'I believe that I have the authority to keep Delacroix house and *all* its properties in good order, without recourse to your uncle. It shall be done,' he paused, 'Might I propose something to you, Miss Delacroix?'

She nodded graciously, still sitting stiffly on her chair.

'While the work is done on the cottage, might you not invite Miss Beauford to London as your companion? With her accompanying you, I feel your aunts might grant you more freedom in London with little fear.'

'It is a good notion, but much as I pitied her, sir, I must say that Miss Beauford was even sillier than my aunts.'

Mr Rigby-Price laughed at her from beneath his caterpillar brows, 'your honesty is refreshing, my dear girl. But I have known Phoebe Beauford since she was young and though not exactly sharp in her wits, I know her to be two things you might need in a companion. Both loyal - and *biddable.'*

She gave a laugh, a delightful and unusual sound to emanate from this young lady 'You persuade me, sir. Once I have permission from my Aunt Sybilla to invite her, I shall write to her tonight.' Delphine rose and her lawyer joined her, she buttoned her kid gloves and said, 'Goodbye sir. I look forward to our next meeting.'

Mr Rigby-Blythe shook his head and chuckled when his client had gone. Long had he wished to help her because the beautiful hermitage she had lived in, with her ice-cold mama, had been no life for a young girl. She was allowed in the garden and the village, but the latter only with her mama. He believed she was used for show, finely kitted out like the daughter of the great house - the daughter of a mother whose self-interest was of an order close to madness. They had exchanged some words and many looks over the years, and he had espied beneath her upright bearing a humorous eye and a desperate spirit. But her sense of purpose and determination amused him. He hoped it would not be sold to the first charming smile, the first caressing words that she heard. Yet, after a life such as she had had, how could she fail to be moved by any affection? Hold fast, young mistress, against the suave tongues and dastardly hearts of the Beau Monde.

CHAPTER 2

Sybilla Lynfield sent letters to her sisters directly after the unexpected capitulation of her niece. When once more lamenting, over her excellent dinner, that Delphine had nothing fashionable to wear for the Castlereigh's ball. It was at this event that Delphine was to be launched onto the world, a world that was already talking about her, anxious for the sight of the most eligible girl in London.

'I really can't take you in a gown that I might have worn at my own come-out, more than twenty-five years ago,' she wailed again.

Her husband raised his eyebrows. His wife's come-out was rather more than twenty-five years ago - he remembered it well. Mrs Lynfield frowned him down. This was no time for her husband to remember anniversaries.

'Very well,' came a bland reply from her niece, continuing to eat her *salmon au crème.*

'You will?' cried her aunt, 'Oh my dear!' She stood as though to run to her, but was put off by the raised eyebrow and cold eye of her niece. Never mind, she would not allow her to retract. She and her sisters would press home their advantage and make her over in a trice.

She smiled and retook her place, countless plans for the morrow jostling in her head. She gave her niece another appraising glance and noticed a gleam around her face she had not before noted.

'What is that at your temple?'

Delphine's hand rose there. 'Oh, is my colour showing? I have need of another rinse, but I do not know how my servant made it, so I have quite forgotten it.'

'What colour is your true hair?'

'Why, blonde, like my papa. It was the greatest trial to Mama. She said it reminded her of her loss, so it was rinsed from the age of seven.'

I did not think that I had the power to be shocked at the actions of Emilia any longer, Mrs Lynfield wrote in the postscript to her sister Eloise, Lady Carswell. *The girl has the almost silver blonde hair of her papa, I had assumed it had darkened since her childhood - but Eloise had it rinsed to a dull brown. So that she would not be reminded of her loss, said she to Delphine, but I believe it was to stop her daughter being her rival in beauty. The poor child. She is still cold, but despite myself, I warm to her.*

#

In addition to her three aunts, Delphine was surrounded by women. She stood shivering in her shift, whilst a number of women pulled her gently about this way and that. Her hair had caused a sensation. It was still damp and hung down her back to her buttocks whilst each aunt and a few of the maid servants lifted it to better see.

'Why it quite lovely, my dear - never have I seen this silver shade in my life, apart from on your papa,' said her Aunt Marguerite

'Like an angel!' said Aunt Eloise.

Delphine had seen herself in the glass after the astringents had been applied to her hair several times, each time washing away more of the dull brown. She was not sure it was so beautiful - it looked odd to her after so many years of the brown. She did admit that her eye colour made more sense than before, but apart from that she had no idea what the fuss was about. Thankfully her lashes and brows were darker, as otherwise she would have looked like a ghost.

She was being very patient. She supposed she had been touched more often in the last half hour than in the previous six months of her life in Delacroix House. It almost hurt her, and the desire to flinch away was nearly overpowering, but she was, if nothing else, a disciplined person.

Now ladies passed tapes around her body and discussed fabric and style as though she were not present.

'I took the liberty of bringing some dresses-,' said Madame Godot, a little French dressmaker, indicating a pile on the bed.

'No, no,' said Aunt Marguerite, Lady Pelleter, 'she cannot wear anything off the shelf - she must have creations made only for her-'

'She needs something or other to wear just now, Mags,' said Aunt Sybilla, 'We cannot even walk to the milliners until she has something more fitting.'

And so it was that Madame Godot stole a march on the other dressmakers present. She shook out the first dress, a quiet muslin with roses on a yellow ground, very simply draped "*à la jeune fille*" said Madame.

The noise around her rose again as her aunts clucked and discussed the colour and style.

'No,' said Delphine. The company froze. She had been silent before this. 'Yellow does not become me.' She moved to the pile on the bed, 'Not the cream ground, but the white,' she said casting the cream to the floor, where a maid rescued it, 'The lavender, but not the olive,' again it was cast, 'I am not sure about the blue.' She pulled it in front of her and looked at her frozen companions.

'She is perfectly right!' Madame Godot was the first to recover from the spell, 'the blue certainly, but not those warm colours with that so-beautiful hair.'

The swarm reasserted itself, and bolts of fabrics suitable for day and evening wear were draped over her, and she could hardly distinguish the sounds or the people from one another.

Her hair was cut at the front a little, and hot irons applied to make curls around her face, her long hair piled and made into ringlets in the classical style so popular. Finally they lowered the pale blue muslin with the hundred tiny ribbon bows at the hem, over the lightest shortest corset she had ever worn, and voila!

Her image in the glass was strange to her and she said, 'How does one not freeze?'

Her aunt Eloise, dropped her own handsome fringed shawl over her niece's shoulders. The semicircle of eyes behind her looked satisfied.

‘She will be besieged, I daresay!’ breathed gentle Aunt Eloise.

‘There is no doubt that men, eligible or not, will fall at her feet!’ said the cynical Lady Pelleter. ‘We shall have to take care.’

Delphine had met the dissipated Lord Pelleter. She did not think that she could trust her aunt to take care. She would have to consider this herself, in the unlikely event that they were correct about a successful debut for her. She had borne enough. ‘Might I be alone now?’ she said coldly.

‘Oh, no, my dear. Monsieur René, the dancing master, is arriving within the quarter hour. And poor Miss Beauford is in the drawing room awaiting you. And this afternoon, now that you are suitably dressed, we might all venture out to the draper’s halls.’

‘All?’

‘Why certainly, all. My sisters are to luncheon here.’

‘Very well,’ sighed Delphine, beginning to regret taking advice from Mr Rigby-Blythe.

#

‘The Castlereigh’s ball! Today we shall see Miss Delacroix and one of her amusing dresses. Lady Scott let me know about a velvet cloak full five miles wide that she wore in the street the other day.’

‘Not really!’

‘Absolutely, it was too opulent even for an opera.’

‘Well, not long now.’ The speaker made a toast, ‘To all of us desperate bachelors with those hounds of debtors baying at our heels, might the best of us be successful!’

The four gentlemen laughed and toasted with him, one shrugging and saying, 'Why do the rich ones have to be oddities to boot?'

'The price we pay, my cynical friend, for a life of ease and plenty.'

#

Delphine, still wearing the pale blue dress, marched into the room that held the timid Miss Beauford with an obvious air of getting on with it. Miss Beauford rose politely, but by her enquiring look, obviously did not recognise her benefactress.

Miss Delacroix herself held a hand out on this occasion, a custom she feared she must adopt, 'Delphine Delacroix,' she said helpfully.

Miss Beauford, engaged in bobbing a curtsy, said, 'You - Miss Delacroix? But your hair is-'

'Different, beautiful-' she said wearily, 'so I've been told.' She was engaged in regarding Miss Beauford critically. Her dress was simple and grey - and unmistakably woolen. She wore crisp white linen beneath, but there was no escaping the mud marks at the hem - the price of travel, of course - and the obvious beginning of fraying. The boots were worse. 'This won't do at all.'

She moved to the door. 'Fiennes!' she called to the butler. He appeared like a genie at her side. 'Have the dress makers left yet?'

'I believe they are packing, Miss Delacroix.'

'Send them.' She said. She returned to Miss Beauford who was blushing.

'I assure you, Miss Delacroix, I do not expect you to buy me a gown-'

'It has been explained to you that you are here as my companion?' interrupted Delphine. '-and you agreed?'

'Oh, I am so happy to do so. A trip to London! You can have no notion how much of a treat-'

'So do you wish me to look ridiculous? Will you stand beside me at a ball in that-' Delphine's hands gestured to the woolen dress.

Aunt Sybilla bustled in. 'What is it you want with the dressmakers Delphine? Monsieur René is even now setting up in the drawing room-' She turned and smiled at the little lady, 'Hello again, Miss Beauford, it is so lovely to see you once more.' Her aunt lowered her voice a little as she turned once more to her niece. 'And what is I heard you say as I came in? Companions do not usually attend balls with one. You have your aunts for that.'

Delphine's eyebrows rose and she looked over her aunt's shoulder to the little woman, who was by now very uncomfortable. 'Do you have any objection to dancing, Miss Beauford?'

'Well no, as a girl it was one of my delights. But I haven't-'

'No matter. My companion,' she said to her aunt firmly, 'will accompany me to balls as well.'

The butler opened the door to the four dressmakers.

'Well, ladies. We have fifteen minutes, I believe, to plan Miss Beauford's wardrobe for the season. She will go wherever I go, so I believe will need everything I need for the season. All the incredible amount of differing things you have persuaded me I shall need, she will need too, I suppose.'

The dressmakers, delighted, came forward to surround the frightened Miss Beauford.

'What are your favourite colours?' asked Delphine above the hubbub around Miss Beauford.

'I wear brown and sometimes grey.' She said, hardly liking to admit she had only two dresses.

'Very well. So green would do too, and perhaps bronze for the evening,' Delphine said speculatively. 'And we shall have to visit a boot maker and - I really cannot be seen with that hat.' She pointed to the sad bonnet on the settee beside Miss Beauford. 'Milliners too.'

Aunt Sybilla who had been frozen by all this, said, 'But my dear Delphine, the expense-' but her niece was headed for the door.

'I will join Monsieur Rene now and you can join us later Miss- I think I will call you Miss Phoebe, and you may call me Delphine - anyway, you seem to have made a start on the dancing, so when these ladies have finished, join me in the drawing room for the lesson.'

She left the room, pursued by her aunt's, 'But Delphine!'

Mrs Lynfield then turned hurriedly to the dressmakers. 'No more than two of each dress type,' she said, biting her lip and regarding Miss Beauford, 'not but what she is right. Make it three. And nothing showy!' She added to the *modistes*. She looked apologetically at Miss Beauford. 'I'm sure you agree, my dear.'

'Oh, quite!' said the little lady.

'So, madam, to be clear,' said the efficient and ambitious little Madame Godot. 'We need three each of morning dress, walking dress, carriage dress, evening gowns and probably pelisses. What about riding habits?'

'Do you-?' asked Mrs Lynfield. Miss Beauford nodded. 'Then I'm sure only two riding habits will suffice.'

'Half dress? Ball gowns?' asked another lady.

'I suppose so.'

'So that will suffice-?' asked Madam Godot her voice trailing.

Mrs Lynfield was anxious to follow her niece before other ructions occurred, so she moved to the door. 'Oh, I suppose you are right, Madame Godot - four of each it is.' She waved a hand and left.

She put her head round the door again to see the women surround the fearful Miss Beauford, and said, in a determination to be frugal, 'But some of them, you know, might be models you already have.'

'*Bien sûr*, Madame,' said that pattern-card of frugality, Madame Godot, struggling to keep the laugh from her eye.

#

'There she is!' hissed Hildegard Sharpe into Gascoigne's ear. His lordship gave a pained expression, but nevertheless turned to see the new arrivals and his heart dropped. It was worse, much worse, than he had anticipated. Indeed, he intended to ring The Honourable Foggy Carswell's neck. How could this poor dab be described as 'quite pretty?' It was beyond even the gleam of her gold to make her so. Her face was a flat dinner plate with a pair of frightened pale eyes regarding the room and her hair styled in the plainest style permitted, a simple coil behind her head. The amber dress they had persuaded her into was indeed more fashionable than had been described, but it was too young for her (what age was she? She had not seen twenty for very much longer than he had been assured) Could he? He thought of the drawer of bills in his study and stepped forward.

As he did so, Sybilla Lynfield moved aside and he saw the third member of the party, a young lady engaged in shaking out a skirt that her male companion, Mr Edgar Lynfield, appeared to have stood on. The dress was certainly from Madame Godot's establishment, it had adorned a form there for some months, its richness and the discreetly whispered price had drawn much attention. The blush silk, and soft silver net worn over it, had a flat, narrow front drape (to emphasise a slender frame) widening to a short train at the back. Cecile, the French dancer he had taken to Madame Godot's, had begged him for it, but he had held fast. Madame Godot had removed the tall stiffened lace collar, which Cecile had so admired, so as to make it suitable for a young debutante, but only just. It was unquestionably the richest gown in the room. Now the girl who wore it stood unnaturally still, her neck and shoulders rising from her wonderful dress, her pale face framed becomingly with silver curls, her serious turquoise eyes meeting his. The Snow Queen of legend, those eyes almost without expression.

He gave a jolt and forgot to look bored. The eyes did not move, the eyelids did not flutter down in maidenly modesty. She looked on. Eventually, not taking her eyes from his, she leaned sideways to whisper to her aunt - for he saw all the traits of the Beauford aunts in her face and knew this to be Miss Delacroix - and muttered something. The aunt looked and muttered something back, something that made Miss Delacroix draw back and turn to her other companion. It didn't halt his purpose, however, his reputation may go before him, but many an inexperienced young lady was attracted by a rake.

He found Hildegard at his shoulder as he marched forth, the younger man hailing Mr Lynfield in a friendly fashion, begging to be introduced to his companions.

Lynfield, dressed for this evening with elegance and precision, sighed, looking at him wryly. 'Well, I suppose so,' he intoned with little enthusiasm. 'This is Miss Beauford,' both gentlemen bowed slightly to the embarrassed lady in amber, 'oh - and Miss Delacroix. Mr Hildegard Foster and Viscount Gascoigne of Raith etc. etc.'

'Etcetera?' enquired Miss Beauford, who had a logical mind, after bobbing a curtsy.

'Oh, there are a number of other titles. I should really give him all his honours, you know - but I have known him long enough to have forgotten them,' said Mr Lynfield, rather bored.

'Miss Delacroix, how beautiful you look this evening.' Hildegard Foster bowed low over her hand.

'Yes,' said the still Miss Delacroix, only turning her eyes towards him.

Her aunt gasped, then trilled falsely, 'We were jesting that we all look very handsome this evening - dressed for the occasion, you know.'

Her husband looked at her piteously, 'Quite. Are you gentlemen here to demand dances? We are blocking the door somewhat.'

Miss Delacroix raised her head to the viscount, but he had grasped Miss Beauford's hand and kissed the air above it, 'May I lead you to the set that is just starting?'

Her uncle raised an eyebrow to Delphine, while her aunt gasped. 'And so it begins!' he said laconically.

'Oh, sir - I mean your lordship. A quadrille! I will need you to mark my steps. I have not much danced these twelve years!'

'Miss Delacroix - may I?' Hildegard Foster was quick when she nodded her head and they moved towards the dance together.

The viscount noted that she did not look at Foster more than the dance dictated, she appeared to be counting her steps. The reason was whispered by his partner, Miss Beauford in a panting voice, 'My cousin and I have only just had a dancing master teach us the quadrille - excuse my poor timing, your lordship.'

'You dance charmingly, Miss Beauford!' she gave a trill of laughter, and he looked up to see if her cousin noticed. It appeared she did not. She seemed to be having a desultory conversation with Hildegard, only answering in single syllables.

As the dance steps led him close to Edgar Lynfield, his eye was caught, just as his hand grasped Miss Delacroix's in the turn of the dance. It was an ironic look that Lynfield gave him. Perhaps the claiming of Miss Beauford to distinguish himself from all the fawning rattles that would no doubt pay the heiress court this evening was a little obvious as ploys went, but it often worked. He glanced occasionally in her direction, but was never rewarded by her regard. His charms must be failing him.

But later that evening, as she stood in a circle of admirers who all sought her attention, he was rewarded by catching her eyes following him. He inclined his head a little, letting a long lazy smile curl his lips, but she neither looked away nor blushed, only stood very still until Nigel Stanhope put his hand on her arm to claim her attention. She recoiled and gave Stanhope a look that might have rivalled that of Medusa. She did not like to be touched.

He danced with another few young debutantes, some of his friends' wives, and meandered around the ballroom talking to acquaintances and laughing with friends. At all times, he now felt her eye upon him. Inside he was smiling. Before he left he would wander to her side and bid her a casual goodbye, exciting her interest just enough.

He would be the counterpoint to Hildegard and the others who had set up court around her, and it would intrigue her.

Robert Duncan, another of his cronies, wandered over to him. 'What have you done to Miss Delacroix, you reprobate? All she did during our country dance was ask questions about you. The queerest sort of questions too. Her aunt had apparently warned about the obvious. And I heard her asking Lady Carswell about you, too.'

Gascoigne yawned. 'I had no idea I was so interesting. But we should be glad for her sake that her aunts have been diligently warning her off my empty purse.'

'I shouldn't think that's all that Mags Pelleter has warned her off. She's an outspoken woman Lady Pelleter. And you thrive on young ladies being warned. Makes you more interesting.'

As he wandered off, Gascoigne moved through the ballroom in the general direction of the heiress, who had taken her seat beside her companion on a bench by the wall, and waved away any gentlemen who came near. It was not a gesture in a debutante's usual behaviour. It amused him. You could not say that she gave herself airs, it was just a plea for some peace.

He wondered if he would be similarly dismissed, but doubted it. She saw him arrive and held his eyes with those extraordinary turquoise eyes.

'Ladies, I take my leave of you. I trust your first ball was a pleasant one, Miss Delacroix.'

Miss Beauford began to chatter and Delphine Delacroix raised her hand to stop her.

'Sir, will you call at nine tomorrow in Russell Square? I wish to speak with you.'

Gascoigne was in danger of showing his surprise. He pretended hesitation, then, 'Of course!'

Miss Delacroix rose, gesturing Miss Beauford to her side. She walked away from him and did not look back.

#

Titus Gascoigne regarded himself in his shaving mirror appraisingly. What did this odd young woman want with him? He was reported to be handsome, of course, and he looked closely. Hair worn a little long and allowed to fall over one eye, the colours, said a woman friend, of autumn. A long face with merry hazel eyes, a hawk nose and a strong jaw. It was his smile, which he reserved for occasions, highlighted as it was with deep dimples, which gave him the universally agreed epithet "handsome". He dispassionately agreed. His charm with women, and his ability to push and pull in the game of flirtation was legendary. Had he been able to bring himself to the mark, he might have married several rich young ladies, whether or not their Uncle Edgar had warned against him. Even because of it. But thankfully a horse had come in, or he'd had a win at Faro in the nick of time to let him escape the married state. *The Wed or Dead League* of gentlemen had been formed in the realisation that for all of them, a win on a horse could no longer suffice. Marriage was the only road to solvency left. That or sign up to the regulars. But a fragment of ball that still resided in his shoulder, plus a gouge in his side was enough to remind him that his debt to King and Country was paid.

He had been a good soldier, he'd unexpectedly discovered. Brought up by two heedless, hedonistic parents, he had become a hedonist himself and had long ago outrun everything but his entailed property. He'd meant to do better than his father, to tend to the huge estate in Shropshire, to put the evils to rights, but the task had seemed beyond him. But the risk and adventure of the army suited him, and even the dark sometimes damp nights under canvas in the Peninsular had a camaraderie about them that he enjoyed. He had always been a leader of men.

And now, the only men he led followed him in manners, and how to tie a cravat. His own careless tie had become fashionable, which could not but amuse him.

There was also the loose association, formed at late night in a tavern, of *The Wed or Dead League.*

There had been six men at the table in Cribb's Parlour that night, when Lord Grandiston had dropped a purse onto the table in passing.

'You winnings Marquis, your time still stands. I got caught behind a cursed cart.'

The gentlemen at the table raised their glasses in a toast to their companion, the darkly handsome Marquis de Chabernet, who pocketed the purse with a Gallic shrug. 'Merci, mes amis, *but this one purse will not save me, I fear. I must marry well and quickly, or die, I think!'*

'So dramatic, Pascal,' had said Gascoigne, 'you must have another!'

'Les Francais sont dramatique, oui, *but also practical. I am at an end in London. I could run, but only as far as this purse would take me. And what then? As well blow my brains out.'*

'That bad?' asked Lord Jeremy Lockhart, his large frame slumping at the same time, 'Fie! It is the same for me. The wolves are at the door, and it is of no use to apply to my father. He's worse than I am.'

Gascoigne stirred, 'You talk of marrying well. Did I not see you dance with Miss Frobisher last evening?'

'You can't say that's marrying well,' said the red haired Honourable Daniel Galbraith in the corner of the booth, 'Her father's a cit.'

'Then the Marquis' ancient name' (for the Marquis had been saved from the jaws of the guillotine as a child, rescued in a potato cart, so it was said), 'will confer on her's some distinction. And she *has ten thousand a year, I believe. And that will bestow equal distinction on the Marquis.'*

'I'm willing, but it is of no use, her papa and two brothers already warned me away. They are not quite gentlemen, but one must admire their style.'

'Gretna!'

'No. Special license, she's twenty-one isn't she? So she does not need her papa's consent. I have a bishop in the family. Here - you're not Catholic are you?' said Hildegard, brushing his fair hair from his face.

'No.'

'Could you persuade her?'

'I think she is disposed to like me.'

'Then you shall be married within the week.'

The Marquis sat at sudden attention, hope on the horizon. 'But I will not be able to get near her.'

'At a crush like the Heston's Ball? Leave that to us, my friend,' said Hildegard Foster, eyes shining.

'Marry well or die. Wed or Dead, I think that is the situation of every gentleman here,' said Gascoigne, getting - a trifle unsteadily - to his feet and raising a glass, 'To the Wed or Dead League, *gentlemen. We pledge ourselves to aid each other in our quest to marry. And the Marquis is our first attempt.'*

'Like the Irish Abduction Club *of last century - they who abducted their brides?' asked Galbraith.*

'No woman shall be abducted against her will. We are English, and have rather more address than that,' said Gascoigne aloofly. 'No, we shall persuade our own young ladies, but the League will do all it can to confound the vigilance of families, who have a prejudice against men who seek their fortunes in marriage. We may be fortune hunters, but we are gentlemen.'

'Wed or Dead!' toasted each in turn. They called for paper and pen and the rules of the league were spluttered onto the paper in increasingly shaken hands. Thus was the inception of the League, and it went forward to this day.

The desperate bunch had almost signed their drunken pact in blood, dedicated to help each other storm the respectable defenses of their female targets. He supposed it was despicable, but he was not troubled by guilt. Each of the brotherhood of *Wed or Dead* was a man driven to marriage as a last defense. All meant to keep to the bargain of marriage as the *ton* dictated - perhaps not faithful, but always discreet in their affairs. To a man they decided to swear off gambling. At least its excesses. And whoring, at least its excesses. He himself intended to be a model husband, at least as far as his innocent wife would know.

The agreement was in a locked drawer in his desk.

Article the First: The gentleman would make a claim on an heiress to the group.

2. In the event of more than one claim on the same lady (quite often the case in these desperate days) the group entire will decide, by careful attention at social functions within the next fortnight, which one has the best chance. The others will then retire from the fray.

3. All the members of the League shall do what is requested by the pretender to the hand to forward his suit - and foil his rivals.

4. A successful gentleman will remain a member for six months after marriage, still pledged to help his brothers.

5. Absolute secrecy is demanded.

6. New members for the League may be suggested, but must be vetted by all the members before joining. Rattles and other such crass gentlemen are never to be admitted.

Next month, member Jeremy, Lord Lockhart, was to marry Maxine Dawson, heiress to a wealthy country squire. Miss Dawson was quiet and somewhat plain, but it was obvious to Gascoigne that it had become a love-match. Engineering ways that Lockhart had been able to meet the carefully tended Miss Dawson had stretched the members' creativity to a great degree, but after a number of meetings, the fish was hooked. In a stand-out fight with her papa, Miss Dawson had been determined in her choice of *fiancé*. She calmly threatened a Gretna marriage if her parent did not agree. Lockhart's eyes shone as he told this story. He was so proud of his bride-to-be.

Deville's case had been messier. A flight to the border with young Lady Harriet Conway, with her brother in hot pursuit and a sword fight in Gretna. In the end her injured brother had served as best man as the two married over the blacksmith's forge. Lady Harriet was a pert young lady, and Gascoigne seriously doubted which would rue the marriage, his friend or she.

Should he now claim his first pursuit? The richest girl in England, the enchanted, but cold, Snow Queen? He knew Hildegard and some others might make the claim also, however his invitation today surely ranked as evidence of his prior and better claim.

#

The purse of pin money that Mr Rigby-Blythe had pressed into her hand as she left him was proving useful. A large coin pressed into the hand of Fiennes had ensured that Viscount Gascoigne was admitted to the library where she awaited him, in a house where only the servants were yet awake. Fiennes had been supremely uninterested in the coin, of course, hardly noticed it in his hand, but had been moved to make a remark.

'Will Miss Beauford be with you, Miss?'

'No. I wish to speak to the viscount on my own.'

Fiennes coughed. 'The viscount's reputation-' he began.

'I understand completely, Fiennes. You can stay in the hall for the duration of his visit, if you must, and should there be a problem I have only to call. I hardly think the viscount would offer me any insult in a gentleman's house.'

Fiennes thought so too. His mistress would not like it, he knew, but there was nothing of the love-lorn about this strange young lady.

Viscount Gascoigne was introduced into the library and found his summoner seated in the peculiarly upright manner he had noticed on the previous evening. She did not rise, but indicated a handsome leather chair opposite her and after the smallest of bows, he sat.

Delphine considered him. She had learnt what she could of him last night.

Her aunt had underlined his terrible reputation with women, had said his pockets were "all to let", had warned about fortune hunters.

Her uncle had taken issue with this label, and he had challenged his wife to name an heiress Gascoigne had pursued for her money. She could not, but merely said, 'Perhaps he has waited for a prize he would consider worthy of his greatness. The Gascoignes have always been proud. And now Delphine-'

'Perhaps! His reputation is founded on a few girls with whom he danced and gave rise to speculation.'

'And the rest!' said his wife tartly.

'Affairs with married ladies are as much their fault as Gascoigne's, don't you think?' Her uncle had said this in low tone, but Delphine had excellent hearing.

Later she had asked her uncle if he liked Gascoigne. Mr Lynfield raised a brow. 'As to his dealings with women, I do not know if I can vouch for his behaviour. Unlike your aunts, I do not concern myself with gossip. But as to his dealing with gentlemen, he keeps his word and aids his friends, and that suffices. Besides that, he is an amusing companion.' He looked down at her with a rare frown and a wagged finger, 'But do not fall in love with him, my dear. He is, as your aunt guesses, something of a scapegrace.'

It was a pity she had not the time to verify her investigations (she had talked to each aunt and every gentleman she had danced with) with Mr Rigby-Blythe. However, it had been borne upon her that she had been somewhat of a hit last night. All her aunts had said so. Being a hit seemed to consist of many eyes regarding one, being solicited for every dance by multiple gentlemen and being paid outrageous complements by complete strangers. None of it had pleased her. For years she had longed for society, to be taken to London and meet a great many people that one would not be forbidden to talk to. However, she had found it far too much all of a sudden. And she had decided something urgent must be done to make life with her aunts comfortable.

Now she looked at Gascoigne who had taken his seat, leaned back, and crossed his legs. He regarded her lazily. It occurred to her that they had not yet spoken - the silence was probably a rent in the fabric of society.

She began with her first concern.

'I understand sir, that among gentlemen you are considered a man who keeps his word.'

Gascoigne gave this start no more than an inclination of his head.

'But it has also been suggested that in your dealings with women the same may not be true.'

Gascoigne did no more than purse his lips at that, a fleeting frown passed his face.

'I have insulted you, I see. I choose to believe that a man who keeps his word behaves the same in all situations. Unless you consider women so far beneath you that they do not merit the same treatment.'

'I do not.' He said it firmly.

'Then I ask at once that what is said between us this morning, whatever the outcome, remain secret.'

Re-crossing his legs was the only indication that Gascoigne was intrigued.

'I give my word.'

'Very well. I have a proposition for you.' Gascoigne looked both amused and uncomfortable at this. 'Not a proposal.' He relaxed once more. 'I have lived a secluded life thus far, sir. How secluded it would be difficult to tell. I need a guide through this world I find myself in, and one who has little interest in persuading me of things.'

'Surely you have been warned, madam, that my purse is empty and yours might just be the answer to my problems.'

'Indeed, I hope it will be.'

Gascoigne sat up at this. 'I thought this was not a proposal, Miss Delacroix. I must say that when I take a wife I would fain chose her for myself.'

'We agree completely, my lord. I offer you not my hand, but employment.'

His laugh rang out loud enough to raise the house.

'Ssh!' she said sternly, 'Or you will cause us to be interrupted.'

'Why me?'

'You are extremely handsome, and have wonderful manners. And intelligence. The tactic of asking my companion to dance instead of me showed much more force of mind than those gentlemen who paid me compliments all evening. I expect if I was inclined to romance, it may have worked. But what it did do was single you out as a better player than all the others. My aunts tell me I know nothing of the world, and they are quite correct. I need a guide to this stormy sea.' She sighed. 'Explaining myself is exhausting. I am really not used to talking so much.'

'If you do not want to be married, what do you want from London society?' enquired Gascoigne with a curve to his mouth. 'What is your plan?'

'I suppose that marriage must be my ultimate fate. But I want to marry on my own terms. I wish to know all that a - a reprobate like you could tell me of my beaux. Whether they are as they appear to a green girl.'

'I have never met such a knowing innocent.'

'I need to know more.'

'You are better, much better, to leave all this to your aunts. They have your best interests at heart.'

'Have you *met* my aunts, sir? Is there a sensible one amongst them? Aunt Eloise was even inclined to be sentimental about *you* - based only on a kindness you did her dog when you were a boy. Naive I may be, but I could see the trap of your charm and your looks at fifty paces.'

Gascoigne's laugh rang out again. 'You are the most original beauty that I have yet met.'

'Very clever, you compliment my looks and wrap it in a jest. It won't work however, and you had best leave off trying. I will never marry such as you.'

He laughed once more. ‘I don’t think I blame you. What next will you say?’

Fiennes entered the library. ‘Miss Delacroix, I should tell you that your aunt has rung for her chocolate. The house awakes.’

Delphine stood at last and Gascoigne knew himself to be dismissed. She held out a folded paper to him.

‘I feared we would be interrupted. Here are my terms, my lord. Read them and meet me in the park this afternoon, say at two of the clock, to let me know if you accept. In any event, I trust you will destroy my letter after having read it.’

He bowed, and Fiennes led him out.

CHAPTER 3

He had ridden to the Lynfield's house, so it was not until he had reached Gascoigne House in Grosvenor Square that he could tear open the seal and read what the remarkable Miss Delacroix had called her 'terms'.

He stopped only to discard his long driving coat and his hat and to pour himself a cognac from the decanter on the side. He was determined to be amused at forming some part of her fantastic scheme, but knew himself to be even more intrigued.

My lord Gascoigne,

I wish to lay my bargain before you with all openness, I beg you will consider my offer as you would that of a gentleman of your acquaintance who offered you such. Consider dispassionately, taking only your honour into consideration, as I do. In this, you may already know, my opinion is based on my uncle, Mr Lynfield's assessment of your character, and as he is the most intelligent of my relatives, I repose the utmost confidence in it.

Your duties, under the terms of this bargain, are to guide me through the dangerous waters of the Beau Monde. I trust my instincts, but it would be useless to suggest that I am experienced in the ways of the world. I could see at once that you are.

Why not leave all this to the attentions of my family? It might interest you to know that I had not met a single member of my family before the death of my mother three months ago. They are kind, and mean the best no doubt, but already they chose what to tell to me, and I trust you will not. I have been compelled to trust another's judgment all my life, and I have found it to be hollow. I cannot again trust to others, at least not without all the facts.

I think that, if it would not incommode you too much, you must pose as a casual pretender to my hand. Or perhaps just as a more casual flirt - you must advise me on this, I do not know what is permissible. This would allow you to keep me abreast of your opinions (which I may or not agree with - my aunts indicate that I am almost as obstinate as my mother). You might take me up in your carriage, or dance with me at balls and so on. In extemis, *we may meet at the British Museum, where we will certainly not see any of my relatives - all of them gaped at me as though I were an oddity when I ventured to suggest I would like to visit.*

Every few days I will send you some indication of my Aunt Sybilla's social obligations for me and I would hope that you might also attend many of these functions so as to regard my suitors - and my demeanour, which I know my aunts despair of. I have been quite alone for most of my life, you see, and so I do not yet know how to engage in light conversation or deliver smiles as other young ladies do. Some of them seemed demented to me this evening, and I find it hard to judge who to base my behaviour upon. You must advise me here.

I have read this letter back to myself, and I quite see that the burden upon you is heavy. It requires a commitment of time you may find onerous. You shall judge if it is worth your trouble. I regarded you closely last evening and saw no attachment manifested to any of the many ladies present (even the married ones - whom my uncle indicated are your preferred flirts) so I hope that our pretend connexion will not disturb some prior arrangement.

You were, this evening, of all the men I observed, the man most at home in the Beau Monde. And thus I fixed on you as the person best placed to help me.

Your reward? First, make a list of your most pressing creditors and send it to my man of business, the attorney Mr Edward Rigby-Blythe, of Beltane Buildings. A note to me before you do so will activate my instruction to him. I say the most pressing, my lord. By all accounts your debts are enormous (source: my aunt Marguerite) and Mr Rigby-Blythe would be unable to hide such sums from my guardian. However, I intend to be a most expensive young lady and this is what the world expects of me. I think that among the dresses, horses and carriages I mean to buy, my attorney will be able to hide our arrangement. In addition to your immediate relief, I trust a sum of two hundred pounds each month might suffice. I heard from Mr Preston last night that you have been known to drop as much as a thousand pounds at the gaming tables upon occasion. I suppose you will have to stop. I simply cannot afford it until I marry.

The butler, engaged in removing the viscount's coat from a chair, was surprised to hear his sharp laugh ring out, before he once more perused his obviously fascinating letter.

Finally, if I become engaged to a suitable gentleman by the end of the season, upon my marriage I will ensure that you receive a sum of five thousand pounds, which I imagine might be easily lost in the cost of my trousseau.

This last, I am aware, is a test of your honour. To receive the final sum you may be tempted to lead me to an unsuitable match. However, either I trust you or I do not. And I have made my decision.

In anticipation of your reply,
Yours faithfully, my lord,
Delphine Delacroix.

#

Cognac in the morning was a bad sign and Burton, who often marked the quantity in the decanter for reasons all his own, noticed that his lordship had made an innings into it. He indicated that he intended to drive in the park this afternoon, and Burton saw it as his duty to ensure that his luncheon consisted of victuals that would tempt him to eat. He removed the brandy bottle to a side table and when he saw his lordship deep in reverie, he took it upon himself to say that full dishes returned to the kitchen were liable to set up Antoine's back and nobody wanted that.

The viscount, aware that keeping the best chef in London waiting for his wages was a delicate job, began to eat his duck, to Burton's relief. In no time it seemed as though the viscount could fancy some rare beef, some *gratin dauphinoise*, a side dish of mushrooms, half a trout cooked with almonds, and some blancmange. As he left the house, whatever demon had possessed his master was gone, and Burton saw him descend the steps to his carriage looking like the handsomest man in London once more, as little Lily the chambermaid accurately remarked.

The general admiration of the viscount extended to his household, or why else would they continue to work for him? He was irregular in his payment of wages, but that was to be expected. Because my, wasn't he the man about town? And were they not all proud to be around his magnificence?

Burton and Mrs Chapel the housekeeper had known him since a baby, Antoine respected the ambition of his table, his coachman and grooms admired his skills with horses, and his man Gregory had served with him in the Peninsular War and talked of his bravery. In addition, every female in the house lived for his lazy smile and his word of praise. Eventually he paid, and none but Burton and Gregory knew that this trust might this time be misplaced.

#

Delphine saw the yellow-bodied carriage with the four horses coming for a long time before it stopped alongside her in the long walk in Hyde Park. Miss Beauford was with her, and they had narrowly escaped being accompanied by Aunt Eloise who'd arrived as they left the house, and kindly offered to take them up in her carriage. Delphine refused, saying that her companion and she had resolved to walk and since none of the aunts were partial to this exercise, they were alone when Viscount Gascoigne stopped his horses and offered to take them up.

The groom went to the horses' heads, and Gascoigne jumped down to assist the ladies into the carriage.

'You might have brought a gig so that we may converse in private!' she hissed.

It was a long time since a lady had talked to him so. There was his late mother of course, and his sister, who lived in Italy now, with her Italian poet. It amused him that this strange girl had so little regard for his dignity. Soon however, both were seated - Miss Beauford in the back and Miss Delacroix on the box beside him. She looked a little askance at the distance to the ground, fully eight feet, then clung to the side and straightened herself to the now familiar upright attitude.

'Well sir, and have you resolved?' she said and quite loudly, as the noise of the carriage surely drowned her words from Miss Beauford's hearing.

'I have, Miss Delacroix. And yet, there are some things that I must relate first. Considerations that might affect your intentions.'

Her eyes narrowed as she paid attention, and he glimpsed their turquoise light, quite amazingly blue in the sunlight.

'I do not have, as your letter so frankly put it, a previous attachment to a lady. However, I do have a previous oath, which to some extent might infringe on our agreement.'

'Can you be more specific, sir?'

'I cannot.'

Delphine sighed. 'Will it involve lying to me?'

'It may involve withholding the truth.'

'Well, that is of no use to me,' she said decidedly. 'As well rely on my aunts.'

Gascoigne was beginning to find her self-possession a little annoying, so he whipped over the horses head and caused her to be shaken about as they darted forward. She let out a small cry.

'A low trick, sir.' She said darkly. He was beginning to think Miss Delacroix's instincts had no need for his town experience.

'There is a way out of it, I believe. It is to let it be known that I am indeed a pretender to your hand. Whether this is consistent with my previous oath I have wrestled with all morning. And I can come up with only one answer that will satisfy all. You must leave me permission to pay my addresses to you at the same time as I honestly - *honestly, I say* - give you the guidance and opinions on your other suitors as we go.'

'But this is absurd. I have told you already that you are disqualified from consideration for many reasons.'

'And they are?' asked he, his ready sense of humour igniting in the absurdity of being given his just deserts by a girl barely arrived in town.

'You are a gambler-'

'But you have already forbidden me this vice in your letter.'

'With no hope that you would pay attention. I have read that it is sometimes in the blood.'

'Oh dear,' he said with an air of a pupil being schooled, 'and the other reasons?'

'You are a, a, philanderer. I can see by my aunt Marguerite's marriage that *this* is not to be borne.'

'Well, naturally, as a genuine pretender to your hand, all, em, philandering would cease forthwith.'

'Even with ladies outside our own class? I have read of opera dancers-'

'Though we have not yet decided on a bargain I offer this advice *gratis* - do not mention opera dancers in polite society.'

'Do you not then have an opera dancer or some such attachment?'

'Not at the moment, no. And I thought I told you not to mention them.'

She smiled as though she couldn't help it and he thought the sun was not as bright as she. 'Why do you not? You hardly deserve the title philanderer if you have not-'

'Miss Delacroix. That is quite enough.' He said sternly, then rather spoilt the impression by adding, 'If you must know I cannot afford one. A mistress can be more expensive to keep than a wife.'

She seemed to consider this. 'Well, that is all the more reason not to consider you a suitor. As soon as we were married you would be able to afford one again.'

He laughed - between shock and amusement.

'Miss Delacroix! Trust me when I say that if my wife prove loving and faithful, I would consider myself a cur to betray her. Whoever she may be. But this is a very improper conversation.'

'I expect you would consider that a wife who disagreed with you in your opinions was unloving-'

'No I would not, but this is beyond the pale, madam. What else have you that disqualifies me?'

'You have thrown away your own fortune, my lord, and it seems absurd to give you leave to throw away mine.'

This time when he whipped the air above his leaders' head, both ladies squealed. He controlled his horses and turned his head to apologise to the terrified Miss Beauford whose white knuckles gripped the side of her seat.

'You are angry sir,' said Miss Delacroix after a moment.

'You are right, madam.' He said briefly. And it was not often that he allowed anyone to make him so. He clenched his jaw and then said, 'You do not know what became of my so-called fortune, Miss Delacroix, any more than my friends do. I was heir to entailed property close to ruin, a proud old name and a monstrous pile of debts. It has been my desire that as few people guess this as possible. As you and I may enter into a business arrangement, and as you have been so honest with me, I suppose you must be told.'

'Still,' she said considering, 'You are very expensive. Anyone can see that. Only look at these horses.' She sighed. 'But I know now, by your honesty, that you are *just* the man for my cause. You may do as you will without artifice to woo me - but you must know that you flog a dead horse.'

He had pulled up near the little pavilion where he had found her, and Hildegard Foster sprang from nowhere to aid her descent. 'Dinner tonight, Hildegard?' He said briefly as his friend's merry eyes met his.

'You still have Antoine? Of course!' Hildegard had by this time aided Miss Beauford to alight and he now drew both ladies arms through his.

'*Au revoir*, Miss Beauford, Miss Delacroix. I hope to see you soon.' He whipped the air and the horses sprang forward.

#

That evening, with *The Wed or Dead League* at the viscount's table, Hildegard said tersely, 'Get on with it, Titus!'

There were only six now. Hildegard Foster, the young buck who had inherited virtually nothing from his father except good looks; The Honourable Daniel Galbraith, a fierce rider to hounds with temper to match his red hair, but a smile that enraptured the ladies; Lord Lockhart, his large frame with a little more meat on it than a few years ago, awaiting his marriage to Miss Dawson; and Sir Peter Deville, dark and brooding, having a difficult time keeping his spirited new wife in check. The Marquis de Chabernet now lived in the country with his wife and it was reported that her father and brothers had accepted him fully, seeing his devotion to his young bride, and enjoying the benefits the rank of Marquise gave her (and, at one remove, themselves) in society. In most cases, the Marquise was first in order of precedence at any social function - accompanied by her whole family.

Three left to marry. Himself, Galbraith, Foster. The latter had introduced a new name for consideration to join the club, a Captain Fanshaw Redmond of the Hussars, and all other members had looked at him as if he were apoplectic. Hildegard grew a little defensive. 'Dash it, he's a friend of mine - a good fellow to know in a tight spot.'

Gascoigne knew some from his regiment who would not agree, but did not say so. Captain Redmond led from the rear, it was said. His stroking and petting ways with the ladies, and his loud mouth were all deciding factors. 'No.' Was Gascoigne's answer and 'Never!' said the booming voice of Lord Lockhart. 'It's alright for you-' said Hildegard sulkily, 'You have your bride.' But the name of Captain Redmond was not mentioned again. 'I think, moreover, gentlemen,' had said Lockhart on this occasion, 'that when all of us find our match, for the sake of our wives the club should be disbanded and never discussed again.' There was a nodded agreement.

Gascoigne stood up, raising his claret in a toast. 'Gentlemen,' said he, 'I claim my first target. Miss Delacroix!' He drank a toast. There were groans from several gentlemen around the table.

'Drat it, the richest prize of all. There's no use in putting my hat in the ring also?' said Hildegard Foster.

'Or me?' said the red-haired gentleman at the foot of the board.

'No chance, Galbraith - or you Hildy,' said Lockhart mockingly, 'We all knew that when Gascoigne finally claimed, none of us could compete. The ladies adore him.'

'*I* thought Miss Delacroix seemed cross with you today, Titus,' ventured Foster hopefully.

'A ploy, my boy, a ploy,' said Deville confidently, 'he'll soon have her eating from his hand.'

'Best of luck, Titus old man. However beautiful she is, she's a cold fish. Barely said a word to me during our dance at the ball,' said Galbraith.

'Me neither!' admitted Hildegard Foster cheerily, 'but she seemed to have a great deal to say to you today in the carriage, Titus.'

'Told you so,' said Lockhart. 'Stand gentlemen! To Miss Delacroix and our proud leader Gascoigne. With every help of *The Wed or Dead League*, may he prosper in his endeavour!'

CHAPTER 4

Miss Beauford's adoration of her niece was not quite to Mrs Sybilla Lynfield's taste.

'I confess, Mrs Lynfield-,'that dame began, breathless in her desire to say all that was thankful of her good fortune.

'My dear Phoebe, please to call me Sybilla. We are cousins after all.'

'Only third cousins, as I understand the family tree in my mama's Bible. But you are so generous to say so. Well, Sybilla then - oh dear, that sounds so ill, would you mind if I reverted to calling you Mrs Lynfield?'

It had sounded ill to Mrs Lynfield too, so she graciously nodded her head.

'Mrs Lynfield, is not your dear niece the most beautiful, kind and generous young lady ever to have lived? I felt a tremor in my heart the first time I saw her close up at the funeral. I never liked to look too closely, you know, when she passed in her mama's carriage in the village. Emilia - your sister, would not have liked it. She was so generous in allowing my sister and me to reside in the cottage, but she made it clear that she could not acknowledge us more than was right. To do so might have caused dissent in the village.'

Mrs Lynfield found herself gritting her teeth anew at Emilia's wicked folly. What harm could the occasional kindness to a poor relation such as Phoebe Beauford and her sister have done? If she were human - but Miss Beauford's chatter continued.

'Who could have known that Miss Delacroix would not just acknowledge, but single me out so? Oh, that my dear mother and sister could have lived to see it. To bring me here and cause all these gowns to be made for me. Why, I have never had more than three gowns all at once in my adult life. And now I have so many. And she makes nothing of it, she only says that I cannot be seen with her poorly dressed.'

'Well that is quite true, my dear Phoebe,' said Mrs Lynfield practically.

'I know, but she said I may keep them. Can you imagine how the people at Oakham village will stare? And she insists on another evening gown, which I do not at all need.'

'Well you can hardly wear the same gown to every occasion.'

'But I am to go home in only just a few weeks - with my cottage made snug for me. How wonderful of the dear girl. Whatever she says about it not being *she* who decided it, but her man of business just putting her property to rights, *I* have no doubts. She is the dearest, kindest young lady.' The little dame held a handkerchief to her eyes at this point, and pity caused the good Mrs Lynfield to donate two caps (which she had found did not become her) to the poor lady - which only made her cry anew.

Later that evening, however, Mrs Lynfield shared her concerns with her husband.

'My dear Mr Lynfield, I have been listening all day to poor Miss Beauford singing Delphine's praises. As if the girl was not set up in her own esteem quite enough, we now have a cheering chorus in the person of our cousin. She is grateful for the dresses, the cottage - and even being *spoken* to by the wonderful Miss Delacroix is enough to send her into high spirits.'

'Do you think Delphine so set up in her own esteem?' asked her husband, wearing what Mrs Lynfield called his shrewd look. He was stretched out on one of her dressing room chairs, holding with her new cap of Angoulême lace, negligently playing with it until she might desire to put it on. 'I think that, on the contrary, Delphine holds onto only a shred of self-esteem that has escaped her mother's wicked destruction of her personality. And I think Miss Beauford's adoration is largely unnoticed by Delphine. Like the attentions of every eligible man in London.'

'You are right about my sister's wickedness,' said Mrs Lynfield, shaking her russet curls regretfully, 'the girl has been strangely raised and it is no wonder she is stiff and has no ease about her. And no affection. When I try to kiss her goodnight, she shuns me. It is just that I see her mother's highness of manner, her coldness, and it repels me.'

'However her manner reflects Emilia's, Delphine is not in any way your sister. Emilia's pride was a corruption of the spirit. How we all chose to leave a poor child with her all that time without fighting to have her visit is something we shall have to live with.' His wife sighed. 'When Eloise took Delphine to visit Miss Phoebe, what was her first reaction?'

'Eloise said that Delphine could not believe how her mother had allowed her relatives to live thus.'

'And she has since, according to Miss Phoebe, written to her attorney to put matters right. That is not the work of such a one as her mother. Miss Phoebe told me that Emilia used to visit occasionally, without her daughter. I am sure it was to have an audience for her superiority. She gave the family the cottage for just that reason. To play Lady Bountiful before them.'

'Not *very* bountiful if Eloise is to be believed.'

'Because she did not care. But however cold her aspect, Delphine did. And immediately.'

Mrs Lynfield rescued her cap from his careless fingers and pinned it in place. 'You are always right my dear. Sometimes I see a glimmer of life about her. Even in her stubbornness I see spirit. But it would be so much easier if she would just do as I say!'

Her husband laughed and drew her ample figure into his arms, resting his chin on her cap. 'My dearest dear, all the world should do what you say.'

Mrs Lynfield nuzzled her russet curls into her husband's shoulder and laughed along as his body shook.

#

Viscount Gascoigne's interest in Miss Delacroix was established fully, in the eyes of the polite world, at a *soirée* given by Sir Reid Cameron on the occasion of his daughter Cecilia's come-out. Sir Reid was a widower, whose dedication to his children was considered saintly by some and a little excessive by others. He had not tried, as many women friends had urged him, to find another mother for his young son and daughter, ten and twelve respectively, when his wife had died five years ago. Indeed, he had seemed inured to feminine charms. It was not until the *soirée*, hosted by his married sister, that he felt the rise of the tide once more. For on that evening, he beheld Miss Delphine Delacroix.

She shone, he said later, in the midst of the busy throng. It was a supper party of only fifty or so couples, with a lady of the group ready to oblige with some tunes for the young people to dance to should they wish, and when do young people refuse a dance? His pretty, brown-haired daughter, wearing a new frock of orange sarcenet, was the centre of attention, squired by all the eligible men in turn. Until the arrival of Miss Delacroix and party.

Even Miss Cecilia Cameron's Papa was riveted by her arrival. Delphine's silver hair shone in the candle light and was bounded by only a broad white ribbon. Her face seemed almost elfin to him, and she was wearing a fairy's dress of pale green silk open over a silver shot satin. Some shimmering bracelet adorned her slender arms, a tiny diamond droplet at her ear and he thought he beheld heaven. She turned to her companion, away from the staring eyes, and her high ringlets danced around her. He was lost.

He recognised one of her party, Lady Eloise Carswell, an old friend of his, and he went towards her in welcome.

Miss Delacroix was introduced, Sir Reid Cameron bowed, and vaguely remembered some talk of an heiress. The obliging lady had started the music and he at once asked Miss Delacroix to dance, this being seen as poor sportsmanship by the other gentlemen, who considered he had taken advantage of his position as host to steal a march on them.

Delphine was still a hesitant dancer, but as the country dancing was usually a romp, all was well. Miss Beauford and a Major-General type with military whiskers were also in the set, she giving an energetic performance. After the set broke up, Sir Reid accompanied Miss Delacroix to the supper table and made a plate for her by his own hand. He was eighteen years her senior, a handsome man with mid brown hair, dark intense eyes, slender and of mid height.

'You must meet my daughter, Miss Delacroix,' he said with the assumption of normality. She smiled a trifle distantly, even more like a fairy than before. She belonged to another world, he thought, but he must bring her into his. Below the table he grasped her hand, in a fit of desperation he had never before experienced. 'You are the loveliest sprite I have ever seen,' he breathed near to her ear. She tried to remove her hand, but it was quite trapped and she raised her eyes, not knowing what to do. She saw only madness in his, and recoiled as she did whenever the emotion that had been missing in her childhood appeared on the faces of others. Even poor Miss Beauford's gratitude was uncomfortable for her, never mind a man who had shaken himself and her by the heat of his passion. She was surrounded by people, but never had she felt so alone, for she was caught in a secret trap and short of screaming - which humiliation she could not stoop to - no escape presented itself to her imagination.

'My dance, I think, Miss Delacroix,' said a suave voice at her shoulder and she stood abruptly, causing the baronet to loose her hand at last.

'Viscount Gascoigne - of course,' she replied, and was swept away from her admirer. She took a deep, shaken breath.

'You'd better toughen up, Miss Delacroix, if you are to last the season. Such a poodle as Sir Reid Cameron did not shake you, surely?'

'In the spirit of honesty, sir, I'm afraid he did. He had my *hand.'*

'No!' said the viscount, shocked. 'Your *hand?'*

'You may laugh sir, but it not all what I am used to. And he looked at me so peculiarly.'

'And yet your hand rests comfortably on my arm with no ill effect.'

'You do not look at me as though you want to eat me.'

He gave such a wolfish grin at this that she laughed in genuine joy.

Across the room, her Aunt Eloise raised her head. Gascoigne making her humourless niece laugh? What on earth-?

Then they were on the floor, dancing the cotillion, seldom avoiding each other's eyes, talking in whispers whenever the steps of the dance allowed. Gascoigne, too, laughed at some remark of hers. What amusing conversation did her niece have that she kept secret from her aunts?

In the carriage back to Russell Square, her aunt gently sought to bring up tonight's behaviours, bracing herself for denial, but wishing to see Delphine's face as she questioned her. She angled the carriage lamp a little so that she missed no expression.

'Lord Gascoigne seemed to be amused by you this evening. Dancing twice is seen as no little attention.'

'Yes. He declared himself my suitor this evening,' said her niece calmly.

'Gascoigne? Declared himself?'

'Is that not the term?' asked Delphine, 'he said he intended to woo me.'

'To which you replied?' screeched her aunt.

'That he should wait in line, as there were other gentlemen before him.'

'You did not! You should not notice the other gentlemen.'

'But how can I not, aunt? I have been followed around at every event for a fortnight.'

'Well, you must *pretend* not to notice them.'

'It is very strange.'

'No doubt. Gascoigne is dangerous, child. No matter what he says.'

'I did not find him so. Mr Cameron, on the other hand, I did.'

'I noticed he was much struck. He did not take his eyes off you all evening. But Mr Cameron is a fine gentleman. Kind, and not in need of your fortune. I had by far rather you were wooed by him than by Titus Gascoigne.'

'I expect,' said her niece with what her aunt felt was a deal too much self-satisfaction for a young lady, 'that I shall be wooed by both.'

#

The declaration of Gascoigne's intent at the *soirėe* demanded the full college of aunts and the hindrance of two uncles. It was of no use thinking that Lord Pelleter was interested in more than his own affairs, so that Lady Marguerite had easily disposed of him before arriving, but in the gravity of the situation, Mr Edgar Lynfield, serious for once, and Lord Carswell (his round face, usually so vague in expression, looking mulishly determined) had both refused to be shaken off, both for their different reasons.

'The first thing we must decide,' began Lady Marguerite, 'is whether the girl faithfully reported what Gascoigne said.'

'I have lived with Delphine Delacroix for a month now,' said Mr Lynfield with his usual drawl, 'and I would say she is a very honest young lady.

'A deal too honest,' added his wife, with a sigh.

'Oh my dear, I know!' said Lady Pelleter, nodding her turbaned head enough to make the little plumes attached shake, 'when Mr Fry said her hair was like the moon glow on a babbling brook, she told him that the phrase gave her a very poor idea of his intelligence and an even poorer one of his poetry.'

'Goodness!' cried Lady Carswell, '*poor* Mr Fry!'

'Not but what she is correct,' said Mrs Lynfield dispassionately, 'the boy has not a sensible idea in his head, according to his mama.' She lowered her voice confidentially. 'He has been s*uch* a trial-'

All the ladies looked interested at this titbit, but Lord Carswell's recessive chin wobbled somewhat as he said, with an introductory cough, 'Ladies, perhaps we might return to the matter at – that is to say-.' His wife's reproachful eyes turned on him and both of her sisters' looked astonished. He coughed again. 'Pardon me!' he retreated cravenly, his hand at his snowy cravat as though it were a little tight.

'You are quite right Pinky, my dear fellow,' said Mr Lynfield pacing, 'the point we had reached was - Viscount Gascoigne of Raith is indeed interested in pursuing Delphine.'

'He has a dreadful reputation, of course, but he is *so* handsome!' Lady Eloise sighed. 'And his rank, you know.'

'That is certainly something,' said Mr Lynfield, a little cynically. 'A ruined inheritance as we all know. His debts are legendary.'

'I suppose that need not trouble Delphine.'

'Very likely not,' said Mrs Lynfield, 'It didn't trouble *you* at any events, Mags.'

Lady Eloise *tsked* at this. It was hardly fair to remind Lady Mags of the bad bargain she had made as a young woman. Especially since her iron will had restored some of Pelleter's fortune. She had stopped her husband gambling, borne him a son to inherit, and had him sign away his remaining entailed and unentailed property to the boy (in exchange for the brandy bottle when he was drunk, the popular story went) and managed the estate. It now made a small income, and Mags had enough to present her pretty daughter this season with good hopes of a respectable match and to keep her eighteen year-old son well mounted. Lord Pelleter had enough pin money to buy horses and womanize, but he had to bear that it was widely known who ruled in his home.

'Gascoigne is a hell of a fellow, you know,' mused Lord Carswell, forgetting himself.

'And if it were not for all his vices, my lord, his rank might make him the perfect match. But she has lived such a strange life and we cannot let a man of the world like Gascoigne take advantage of her innocence,' said Lady Pelleter.

'Of course I know Delphine *is* innocent,' mused Mrs Lynfield, 'but sometimes it is hard to remember. She is the most unusual girl.'

'Sybilla!' protested the kind-hearted Lady Eloise.

'We must forbid her to spend time with him, to even dance with him!' said Lady Mags with decision, her black brows drawing together.

'That would be unpardonable. To cut a man of his rank!' protested Mrs Lynfield.

'I thought rank did not concern you?' asked her husband, amused.

'She need not cut him, merely excuse herself politely. Have the headache, or turn him off with some other smiling excuse,' said Lady Eloise, 'Christiana has dealt with the Duke of Clarence and his squeezing hands in this way, and if she can do so with a royal duke-'

'Yes,' said Sybilla practically, 'but Christiana is your daughter, my dear Eloise, and like Mags' Roberta, has been taught how to behave prettily in every situation. Delphine is Emilia's daughter. She veers between stiff silence and surfeit of honesty, no matter what I tell her to do.'

'I know,' sighed Lady Eloise, 'When Benjamin Castle, who was much too old for her, but still sees himself as a young buck, roguishly asked for a dance she looked him up and down with a dead-eye and said "No." That was all, just no. I could not get her to see afterwards what she had done. It was most embarrassing!'

'And yet, ladies,' said the sensible voice of Mr Lynfield, 'she has taken. There is no doubt she has taken. The *Beau Monde* loves her. One could conjecture that her great wealth makes her fireproof, but it is not just that. You ladies made yourselves a masterpiece. Her clothes, her hair have revealed a true beauty in Delphine that I certainly did not espy when I first saw her. Emilia, even in dressing her richly for the entertainment of the village, had robbed her of her natural self.'

'But when she opens her mouth!' sighed his wife.

'It is certainly a problem. Indeed, there is little hope that she could turn off Gascoigne with any kind of style. Even if she wanted to.'

'He is just too handsome,' sighed Sybilla, 'Could you not warn him off, sir?'

'On what grounds? It would be an unpardonable insult.'

'Well, I shall keep a close eye on her,' said Mrs Lynfield determinedly, 'I shall take care that she does not fall across his path.'

The door to the green salon opened, and the company fell quiet as Delphine entered, charmingly arrayed in a blue velvet pelisse and a simple straw bonnet with velvet ribbons, which Lady Eloise had chosen for her just the other day and was happy to see became her well.

'Oh, I did not know you were present aunts, Lord Carswell! Aunt Sybilla, Miss Beauford and I are just going for a carriage ride with Lord Gascoigne. We shall not be above three hours,' Delphine said coolly.

Lady Sybilla's mouth had fallen open, making a perfect 'o' shape as her niece softly closed the door.

The company hastened to the twelve foot high window in a clump, to see Viscount Gascoigne hand first Miss Beauford into the smart barouche, and then Miss Delacroix, bending over her hand as he did so and kissing the air above it.

'Oh dear!' said Eloise Carswell, summing it up for them all.

#

'I feel Mags Pelleter's eyes driving a nail into my head,' sighed Gascoigne with a wry look, as he waved off his groom to start the horses.

'I think your reputation goes before you,' said Delphine. 'I told them you intend to woo me.'

Both Miss Beauford and the viscount uttered a noise, but with a few octaves difference. 'You did what?'

'Well we must announce it to the world, you said.'

'I meant by my actions, not by telling them that I had declared myself.'

Miss Beauford gave another squeak. 'Could it be, is it the case, that you are - are engaged, my dear Delphine?'

'Goodness, no!' retorted Delphine, in a manner Gascoigne felt insulting. 'I suppose we must take Miss Beauford into our confidence a little, sir.'

'I seem to be in your hands, Miss Delacroix,' he sighed.

'Lord Gascoigne and I have an arrangement.'

Miss Beauford trembled.

'Not that sort of arrangement,' his lordship soothed.

Miss Beauford took a breath.

'What sort of arrangement?' asked Delphine, confused.

'Never mind,' said Gascoigne with an ironic lift of his brow,' continue to tell Miss Beauford something, anything, which will stop her looking at me as though I were the serpent of Eden.'

'Lord Gascoigne has agreed to give me advice on society, on my deportment, my behaviour, and so on. And on the true characters of my suitors. I am to use his worldly experience.'

Miss Beauford looked extremely uncomfortable. 'Well I'm sure the viscount has a great deal of experience, my dear-'

'None more,' chirruped the viscount, enjoying himself.

'-but I think you may count on family for the best advice,' she finished apologetically.

'The aunts? Yes, I understand why you would think so. They have a great deal of experience, but I do not know that what they wish for me is exactly what I would wish for myself. They wish me a suitable husband - but look at it as I do, my dear Phoebe. Between them they have wed a fool and a degenerate. My Uncle Edgar is the only sensible choice among them, and with all Aunt Sybilla's silliness-,' here Miss Beaufort uttered a faint protest '-I cannot help feeling she married with a deal more luck than judgment.'

'Oh!-' protested her companion, distressed. But Delphine had not finished.

'Thus I looked about me for a man whose word was to be trusted (my Uncle Edgar has said so of Gascoigne) and moreover, a man who had enough of the usual number of gentlemen's faults to see them in others.'

Gascoigne bore this well, he was becoming accustomed to the cutting honesty that emerged from Miss Delacroix's mouth. Miss Beauford gazed at him timidly, 'Then you are not, as was said, courting Miss Delacroix?'

'Yes,' said the viscount.

'No,' said Miss Delphine.

'You are seeking to woo my cousin? I do not quite understand. Oh dear, how awfully intrusive this conversation has become.'

'Yes,' once more the viscount.

'No,' again Delphine.

'I am confused,' said the poor little lady, wringing her reticule into a tight coil.

Delphine sighed. 'The viscount has declared himself to woo me, like every other fortune hunter in London. But I have told him he would do better to put his efforts elsewhere. I hear Miss Frampton has a sizable fortune. Nothing to mine, says my aunt Marguerite, but enough to tempt many a gentleman.'

Miss Beauford gave an audible gasp. 'My dear, you really ought not to say such things-'

'And I would have to get over Miss Frampton's nose. I do not think I could make love to that nose, you know,' mused the viscount. '-or at least, not convincingly.'

'I expect you could for twenty thousand a year,' snipped Delphine.

'My dear!' protested Miss Beauford, beginning to feel faint.

'Probably,' considered Lord Gascoigne, 'but I do not have to - since I have pledged my heart to yours.'

'You really are a ridiculous man,' said Miss Delacroix, whilst Miss Beauford looked between them anxiously. 'Do not worry, my dear Phoebe. It is his lordship's idea of a jest, I think. He is simply here to advise me.'

'Well my first advice is,' said the viscount, touching his groom to stop the horses as they were near a pretty walk in the park, 'that you never speak of such things in polite society again.'

'But my aunts speak of them.'

'They may among themselves, but young ladies may not. Young ladies do not mention such things as wealth, fortune hunters, and gentlemen's -eh- faults. And especially not in front of the servants. My own servants are constitutionally deaf and dumb,' Here his tousle-haired groom grinned as he held the horses' heads. '-but that is because I threaten to bull-whip them if my business is heard of abroad.' The groom grinned again.

'Well, I shall not do so again. I shall try to ignore that I am solicited for every dance just for the size of my fortune. Or that I fear the vices of men.'

'And still she mentions it. But is it possible, Miss Delacroix,' Gascoigne said in quite another voice, one that gave Miss Beauford the shivers, 'that you do not know you are admired as much for your beauty as your fortune?' His hazel fox eyes met her turquoise ones and Miss Beauford held her breath.

'Well, it is quite impossible for me to know sir, for a fortune I do have.'

The ladies descended the carriage and all three of the company walked along a slender path off the main thoroughfare. There were still blooms aplenty to admire, but Miss Delacroix was all business.

'What do you know of Sir Reid Cameron, sir? My aunts have him a saint, and I did not take to his manner at his daughter's ball, but I do not wish to dismiss him yet, if you know no ill of him.'

'No ill in the world, save that he is deadly dull.'

'Remember, sir, that we are not in pursuit of gentlemen of your stamp.'

Miss Phoebe groaned.

'In that case, he may be the very man for you. He is accredited a wonderful father and was a devoted husband to his wife while she lived, and to her memory when she died. Indeed, until your silver hair was in sight, I believe him untouched by female allure.'

'He didn't strike me as overly intelligent.'

'Agreed.'

'I should wish for a sensible man, but biddable *might* do as well.' Miss Beauford squeaked, but Delphine did not appear to hear. 'What about Mr Fry? My Aunt Mags holds that I was insufferably rude to him, but he may come about.'

'Mr Fry is solvent, if not rich, and a poet. There my information ceases on the subject.'

'Well, find out more, if you please, and let me know.'

This improper conversation was stretching Miss Beauford's nerves to breaking point, but as she could find no way to stop it, she walked ahead, muttering platitudes about the roses.

It was forty minutes before they had finished, and they had covered more than two miles by the little lady's reckoning when they re-joined the carriage. They tooled around a little, with the occupants of the park staring - when was the last time Gascoigne had driven a debutante? - and eventually met The Honourable Linton Carswell, in a hired gig, who held his hand up to hail them. The groom stopped and they were abreast of the gig, looking down a little. The young man looked up, his anxious, diffident demeanour reminiscent of his papa.

'Ho, Foggy? What ails you today?' The viscount noticed that the young sprig's prominent Adam's apple, more obvious as the fair haired young man had no chin, was bobbing up and down in a way that denoted a crisis of nerves.

'Ho, Titus, ladies. Um, my Pa wanted me to offer to take you ladies home now. Um, something about a dress fitting, don't ye know?'

Gascoigne looked disappointed. 'Couldn't you do better than that Foggy? Sent to call me off, are you?'

'Dash it all, Gascoigne-' objected his lordship, blushing.

Miss Delacroix took pity on him. 'I am quite happy to come home now, Mr Carswell,' she turned to the viscount, 'Help me down, my lord!'

'You mean, *pray* help me down my lord,' instructed Gascoigne.

'Yes, indeed!'

Both ladies left the barouche and joined the gig.

'Do you attend the opera tonight, Lord Gascoigne?' asked Delphine, when she was seated in the gig with Miss Beaumont, glad they were both slender.

'Perhaps,' he said, smiling down on her in such an enticing way that Miss Beauford, whose breath was not her own today, gasped once more.

'Do!' her cousin said and then when she perceived the other occupants of the gig stare, added, 'I mean - we shall hope to see you there, Viscount.'

'Much better,' approved Gascoigne with a smile, but Miss Delacroix's eyes were straight ahead, done with him for the moment.

CHAPTER 5

Mr Rigby-Blythe had an unexpected visitor at his offices. The magnificent form of Viscount Gascoigne of Raith arrived, wearing a coat with a great many capes, his tall hat in hand, his curls falling roguishly over one eye, the shine of his boots and the glare of his linen almost startling in the small inner office.

The lawyer had read the card sent in to him, and had some notion of his lordship's business, but still, the whole of him somewhat distressed Mr Rigby-Blythe. He had never seen such a handsome, polished specimen of manhood - how was his inexperienced young lady supposed to resist such a nonpareil? It took only seconds to know that the body before him could dance, ride, drive, and shoot to an inch. His curling lip denoted wit and his exquisite manners, exampled by the depth of the bow: just a trifle more than a lowly attorney merited, which showed respect for Mr Blythe in particular. He feared his young lady was quite lost.

'Mr Rigby-Blythe,' said Lord Gascoigne's well-modulated, honeyed tones, 'I am here to present myself to you, instead of forwarding the papers you may be expecting-' he lifted his eyebrows interrogatively, and the attorney nodded, '-because Miss Delacroix has expressed to me that you have been to her, for many years, a friend. Her only friend, she told me.' Mr Blythe indicated the chair that Miss Delacroix had occupied a week since, the viscount took it and the old man sat behind his desk. 'These debts are pressing, I need not tell you it troubles me to so expose myself to you. But I needed you to see, to have you know sir, that in our strange arrangement, I mean Miss Delacroix no hurt. I am obliged to accept her money in relief of my situation, but I shall not behave dishonourably.'

'A lady such as Miss Delacroix, one kept only to herself in a rich old house, with no affection given by her mama,' Gascoigne's eyes narrowed at this, 'and unable to form even a friendship, may be rather easier to hurt than you can grasp, Viscount.'

'You may peruse my papers, sir,' said the viscount, 'if there is anything objectionable in there, please let me know.' He sat still as the lawyer read.

There were many things of note in the sheaf of bills that Gascoigne included in his pile, some by their absence. To wit, no gambling debts. Either the viscount had stopped gambling, or he didn't gamble beyond his ability to pay. Second, among the stabling, the wages, the tailors' bills etc., the lawyer understood that the viscount ordered his creditors equally. He did not, as most of his class did, consider tradesman's bills beneath his concern.

'This is all?' said the attorney.

'Those are the London debts in their entirety, but there are many claims against my country estate, many predate me. I feel I could not pass that burden to Miss Delacroix. She was quite clear that I should only include the most pressing.'

'In that spirit, what would you judge the most pressing in Shropshire?'

'The wages bill. Many old retainers have not been paid these two years. Also there is a hideous charge for the repair of the roof. Gascoigne Manor is crumbling and when I set the workers to repair, I believed, for reasons that I shall not bore you with, that I would be able to pay.'

'A swift computation of the London bills comes to two thousand guineas only. Miss Delacroix has instructed me to allow five thousand. It will be difficult, to hide such a sum in her allowance, but life is full of challenge.' The old attorney said this comfortably, not doubting his own powers. 'Mr St John Beauford has agreed that I must be generous in the sums needed to set the young lady as the first lady of fashion. He has hopes of a Duke at least as a suitor.'

'The only unmarried Dukes I know, including the Royal Family, are at least twenty years beyond Miss Delacroix.'

Mr Rigby-Blythe, at first wishful to put blockades in the viscount's way, found him honest and winning. 'Let us allow another two thousand for the wages at the manor and the roof. Will it suffice?'

'I had no idea of coming here to extend my sheaf of debts. But if I could pay the Manor's staff I would be-,' he could hardly speak. There was about him an air of humiliation amongst the gratitude, and the old man liked him for it.

'If you will act for her as she wills, you will soon earn your hire.'

Gascoigne flushed. Mr Rigby-Blythe left his seat and went around to lay a fatherly hand on his shoulder.

'If it makes you feel better, my boy, this money is as nothing in the wealth of Miss Delacroix. One set of properties in a hundred will give her that in a month.'

'Very well, sir,' said the viscount, unexpectedly touched by a fatherly gesture that he had seldom experienced, 'I shall not think of it. But Miss Delacroix mentioned a monthly sum.'

'Two hundred pounds, I know.'

'Half of that will suffice. And I do not think you have to relay that to Miss Delacroix.'

'Very well, my boy. But if I know Delphine Delacroix, you will earn that and more as she makes her way in the world.'

The viscount stood, shaken by much that had happened here today, but regaining his old manner swiftly. 'I fear you are right, sir.'

He retrieved his hat and held his hand out to the rusty old attorney as he would an equal. Their hands met.

'Whatever happens, my lord,' said the old man gently, 'I would ask you one thing. Be open and honest with Miss Delacroix. More than most, she does not understand duplicity.'

'I promise, sir.' And his hand grasped the others closely for a second, before he turned in a swirl of coat, and was gone.

#

There was much for the *ton* to talk of in the behaviour of Miss Delacroix and Lord Gascoigne. They seemed to spend much time together: spied driving in the park, enjoying at least two dances together at each suitable entertainment, and affected to meet each other at various times in the street, when Miss Delacroix was shopping, or visiting the lending library. Then there were the chance meetings at the opera, or Vauxhall gardens, or at the play. It was very often that the viscount joined her party, buying supper afterwards for her aunts and her companion, too. There were many vigilant mamas who pitied Sybilla Lynfield. How did one stop a charming viscount, whose family one has known forever, from joining the party?

On the other side, Miss Delacroix was hard to read. Other fashionable debutantes had begun to ape her manners. Be cold and unresponsive - for it seemed to drive the gentlemen mad. She spent time with the viscount, he who had never before wooed a debutante, but she seemed oblivious to his many charms. Quite often as they danced she was seen to frown - certainly, she did not display that overall swooning admiration that other young ladies did in his presence. Also, she danced with many more pretenders, but seeming to jettison certain gentlemen after a time. If she had a favourite besides Gascoigne, it was hard to judge, but certainly some fell from her favour.

The patronesses of Almacks club, which offered dancing regularly without the need for a private ball, could not agree her character. The vouchers were restricted: only given to those of the Beau Monde who could meet their rigorous standards. A whiff of scandal, a hint of vulgarity and you would not be admitted, whatever your rank. On the one hand, her birth and manners were perfection, on the other she seemed frivolous in her treatment of young gentlemen. And she was altogether too self-possessed. Her odd upbringing might account for it, but it upset the status quo. Nevertheless, she was given vouchers for the club (the aunts would have been furious if she had not) at least until the patronesses could decide what on earth was so disturbing about her.

So the weeks passed, and under the guidance of Gascoigne, rather than her aunts, she began to change. She smiled a little more often, unwittingly making more slaves than she knew. Gascoigne had advised her that of all the ladies whose manner he admired, Captain Fraser's wife was the preeminent. She was a friendly and winning woman of thirty or so, whose charm of manner made her many friends. She could be still and reserved in company that did not please her, rather like Delphine herself. She held herself well, but was *never* (and Gascoigne emphasised this) high in manner with her inferiors.

Delphine studied her, and did her best at imitation. 'Oh, Mr Carswell,' she enthused when Foggy came within her orbit at the ball for his sister Christiana, 'how perfectly *wonderful* to see you again!' She smiled and held out her hand in Mrs Fraser's winsome way, and Foggy recoiled, gurgled and then excused himself.

'It is of no use,' said Delphine to Gascoigne, sipping the claret-cup he had brought her as they sat on a small divan at the edge of the ballroom. 'I cannot get it right. My attempts to adopt Mrs Fraser's manner caused The Honourable Mr Carswell to be almost apoplectic.'

Gascoigne smiled. 'Poor Foggy. Well, perhaps the leap from cold autocrat to warm and winning in one move is a trifle unnerving.'

Delphine sighed. 'I shall never be at ease here.'

'Perhaps it is better that you adopt your own style. It seems to serve you well amongst your suitors.'

'I think, don't you, that it would take my producing a pistol to scare some of my suitors away.'

'Do not again curse your inheritance. You desire that the suitors who want your money will go away. And then you suspect the suitors who are moved by your beauty. What do you wish your projected spouse to admire about you?'

She was checked. 'Something in my soul, I think.'

He was silent, looking deep into her eyes, 'And how can they know your soul if you are not yourself?'

'But we agreed that myself was not fit for company, have we not? I am cold and an autocrat.'

'Not always cold.' He said briefly. Delphine flushed and a silence reigned, long enough to become uncomfortable.

'I do not mean to be autocratic, but I saw only one mode of being my whole life.'

'Yes,' he said, 'being autocratic with me, or indeed with your suitors is simply amusing. Men are not used to it, but upon reflection it makes you unique, a character. What I do not like to see, what distresses me, is when you order poor Miss Beauford,' (he regarded that lady who was dancing a reel with gusto) '-or a servant. An altered tone, a kind word to a person beneath you in rank is the mark of a true lady - or indeed of a gentleman.'

The hand that raised the cup to her lips shook and lowered it again to her lap. The viscount grasped it briefly, before she pulled away. 'I did not mean to hurt you,' he said 'I-'

'I know that you are right. Many times when my old habits recur, I see Miss Phoebe crushed - just by a word from me. I was never allowed to show any connection to anyone, you see, was always encouraged to show my superiority of rank.'

'Superiority of rank is an invisible thing. Or it is best so. It comes of careful treatment of those who depend on you.' He grinned. 'Nowadays, that includes me, Miss Delacroix - you must always be gentle with *me*.'

'Pah!' said Delphine, thus able to recover herself, 'being gentle with you would only increase your arrogance.' She did the thing he liked with her serious turquoise eyes, 'we are agreed then, that aping Mrs Fraser, however socially accomplished she is, is outside my talents. I shall be the cold and autocratic Miss Delacroix, and everyone will call me a charming eccentric because I have a hundred thousand a year.' She looked at him full in the face then and when she did this, he found her searing honesty shook him, 'but I listened to you about taking my autocracy beyond the ballroom. I do not mean to hurt others, but you have made me understand that I do. Thank you.'

Gascoigne felt a twist to his stomach as she dropped her eyes. That this girl would thank him for pointing out her failings, he who had sinned so much, was almost insupportable. The wave of self-disgust almost choked him. 'Ha!' he said at last, 'Here comes your clerical admirer. Mr Wright is both rich and holy, and I fear he has learnt the steps of the quadrille.'

'Was not that our dance, my lord?' asked Miss Delacroix regarding the vicar rather desperately.

'I freely give it up to one so much closer to heaven than I,' said the viscount standing, then melting away into the throng.

Delphine looked where he had gone for a moment before she was able to turn towards the gentleman who had joined her. He asked for her hand, and newly true to herself she said nothing and merely followed him to the floor.

#

'Miss Beauford, my dear Phoebe, might you stay a little before you go to bed?'

She gestured away the maid who had taken down her hair and helped into her nightgown and then caught herself guiltily. 'Um, thank you so much, Rose, that will be all for this evening.'

Rose, almost out the door in response to the imperious hand, paused awkwardly and bobbed a curtsy. 'Miss!' and flew away.

Miss Beauford was perfectly willing to oblige, and sat on a small chair opposite Delphine's, at each side of the dying embers of the fire. She looked a trifle nervous and plucked at her night gown.

'Have you ever wondered, Miss - my dear Phoebe - why I asked for you to join me in London?'

'Well, of course there is the cottage that you have caused to be - I really cannot thank you enough for *all* you have done for me. I-'

'Yes, yes,' began Delphine briskly, and as Miss Phoebe's eyes filled once more with anxiety, she caught herself, softening her tone. 'I wished the repairs on the cottage, certainly, but when a friend suggested you come here to be my companion, I was selfish enough to see how it could work for me. With you at my side I have a great deal of freedom.'

'Oh, I am so happy to be of use to you. It has been quite wonderful visiting London again.'

'You visited London before?' Delphine was diverted from her course for a moment, realising that she had never asked her companion a single question about her past. She knew nothing of it.

'Why, I had a season here when I was just seventeen, my dear. I enjoyed it very much.' She saw that Delphine was confused. 'Did you not know how my mama and sister and I came to Oakham? Well, we lived in our Manor House whilst my papa lived, with every happiness, I assure you. My sister and I did not *take* in London, we were rather plain, you see - but we still paid some visits to the town occasionally to see the play or buy some new muslin.' Phoebe looked into the dying embers, 'We were such a happy family - but girls, you know, and after papa died-'

'You did not inherit,' said Delphine.

'No, a nephew of my papa did, and naturally he wished the house cleared of us all. That is when mama applied to Lady Delacroix, her nearest relation. Your mama was so kind as to let us have the cottage. Mama always told us we had to be grateful to her ladyship for her bounty, else we might have starved. But with the cottage and mama's fifty pounds a year all was well.'

'And after you mama died? How did you manage then?'

'Well, mama saved as much as she could each year for just that time. So along with my garden - do you think the workers will be careful with my garden? - I have been quite alright. Of course I have felt my lack of funds a little here in London. It is customary, you know, to give little tributes to the servants on a visit such as this, and I have felt awkward-'

Delphine thought of the produce garden at Delacroix House, the vast glass houses that grew things just for their household. She knew that servants who were found with the fruits of this garden in their pocket or their mouths, beyond the meals ascribed by her mama, were cast off, even if all the excess food rotted away. She said, with a sinking heart, 'But my mama would have sent you some baskets of food from our garden and storehouse?'

'I do not believe so, no.'

Delphine stood suddenly and paced. A rage such as she had never known, never allowed herself to feel, possessed her now and Miss Beauford watched in alarm.

'She visited you. She knew your condition. And yet she-' her voice was rising, 'She was a monster!'

'Oh do not say so, my dear. Without your mama-'

'Oh, she gave, that monster. But everything she gave was *poison.*' She stopped her pacing and looked at little Miss Beauford, whose once sharp bones were now covered in flesh. 'I am not she! I will *never-'*

Phoebe's eyes watered, 'Oh, do not distress yourself, my dear Delphine, you are so wonderfully kind to me.'

'No Phoebe, no,' Delphine cast herself at the little woman's feet and grasped her hands passionately, 'I brought you here to further my own plans. It was all selfishness, just like her. You have shown me affection and loyalty and friendship and Gascoigne has shown me how I have treated you. I am ashamed, Phoebe, so ashamed. You will never be in want again, I promise you, I promise you! And I will treat you better, I *will* - only say you forgive me.'

With this last, Delphine cast her head on Miss Beauford's knee and sobbed. 'My dear girl,' she whispered, caressing her head, 'my dear girl.'

Mrs Lynfield, in her nightdress, with her hair in papers, entered to see what the noise meant. Her eyes met Phoebe's over Delphine's head, she bustled forward putting her arms around her niece's shoulders, 'Come, come, my dear, what ails you Delphine?'

Delphine rose and threw herself into her aunt's arms. 'Oh Aunt Sybilla, I am not her, am I? Tell me I am not her-'

Her aunt, grasping Delphine to her breast at last, did not pretend to misunderstand her. 'No Delphine, you are not my sister, you could never be like her-' she moved her niece towards the bed, Delphine's hysterical sobs catching at her heart. Miss Beauford leapt forward to pull down the coverlet. 'There, there, my dear. Have a good cry then try to sleep. We will see you in the morning.'

Delphine wept into her pillow, large wracking sobs that shook her frame. The two older ladies turned at the door of the chamber to look at her, 'The dam has finally broken,' whispered her aunt. 'She needs to cry it out, I fear-. She didn't mention a gentleman?'

'Only that Lord Gascoigne had said something about her treatment of me, which is quite absurd. She has showered me with kindness, I can never be sufficiently-.'

'Yes, yes,' said Mrs Lynfield, 'but she has been a little curt upon occasion, has she not? Mmm, Gascoigne, what are we to do about Gascoigne?' Considering this question took her hostess to her own chamber, which was just as well, for Miss Phoebe had nothing to suggest.

#

Lord Gascoigne and a number of gentlemen callers left their cards the next morning, but Miss Delacroix was not at home to visitors. It was a pity, but not unexpected. A young lady who had been to every dissipation that the town could deliver in the way of balls, assemblies, house parties, the opera, the play, the park, the dress maker and milliner, would of course give in to exhaustion eventually, thought the world.

But Mrs Lynfield was concerned and had summoned reinforcements in the persons of the aunts.

'What are you *now* wearing, Eloise?'

Lady Eloise looked down at her chiffon bodice with the palest pink silk beneath, cut to the lowest possible point, the colour suggesting that she was naked beneath.

'Oh, the style is all the crack. It is called Eros, I understand.'

Mrs Pelleter waded in. 'As well it might. Surely it is a style for a lady much younger than yourself?'

'And of quite another class!' sniffed Mrs Lynfield, with more than a little jealousy at her sister's magnificent figure.

'You jest, my dears. *Everyone* will be wearing it soon.' Her sisters' eyes met, exchanging a rueful glance. But there was something to be attended to.

Both of them had visited Delphine, still abed, and saw a wan child whose eyes denoted a night of weeping. After a short visit each, they had joined their sister in the morning room, both a little shaken.

'She held my hand and asked my forgiveness!' said Lady Mags.

'She hugged me and said I had always been so kind to her-' said Lady Eloise, just as shocked. 'What on earth has occurred?'

'Gascoigne!' said Lady Pelleter, her brows meeting dangerously.

'No, or not directly. It is something to do with Miss Phoebe and my sister's appalling treatment of her. For some reason - and that may be at Gascoigne's instigation - she has understood that she too is a little selfish with Miss Phoebe-'

'Pooh, the poor dab has never known such luxury. Delphine has treated her just as she ought!' said Lady Mags.

'Well,' said the soft voice of Lady Eloise, 'perhaps she could moderate her tone a little. She barks orders rather than makes requests.'

'But she realised last night that she had not enquired about Miss Beauford's past or really showed any interest in her circumstances-' said Sybilla, patiently.

'Why should she, indeed? It is enough that she brings her here and dresses her and has caused her home to be made cosy,' said the stolid Lady Marguerite.

'Well and Miss Phoebe is very conscious of all she owes Delphine, but said that Delphine had taken it into her head that she was just like her mama, and had hysterics.'

'Well to think oneself like Emilia would drive *anyone* to hysterics.'

Lady Eloise said, 'I think this must do the girl good. Even we worried that she was as cold as our sister, and happily, now we see how wrong we were.'

'But *Gascoigne* once more - what has he to do with any of it and what should we do about him?' asked Sybilla.

'I do not see that in anything but time spent together, Delphine displays any preference for him. Much of the time they appear to be arguing,' offered Lady Eloise.

'But *intimately* arguing - it is most disturbing,' said Lady Pelleter. 'One is polite to enemies and one fights with friends.'

'But not lovers,' said Sybilla, 'or at any rate, not in the early stages. We must hold on to that.' She shook her russet crop of hair, 'St John wrote to me for an account of her season thus far. I have told him of her many conquests - that she is all the rage - and I mentioned Gascoigne.'

'Ah – our brother will forbid such an attachment, of course,' said Lady Eloise, relieved.

'Unfortunately, no. He was Gascoigne's superior officer for two years, and said he was just the fellow for his niece.'

'Men!' said Mags Pelleter.

CHAPTER 6

The landlord at the Three Swans Inn in Gascoigne village was keeping an eye on a certain individual who had taken a room there for the last three days. He was a slimy, insinuating go-by-ground with a face like a weasel and a moleskin waistcoat. He talked a great deal and was free with his money, buying the local dairymen, farriers, or others who frequented this house, tankards of ale - in the most open handed manner possible. He seemed to like to talk and he said he was a journeyman carpenter, taking his ease along the route to a new position and finding the little village of Gascoigne, and the people therein, quite the pleasantest he had encountered. But the landlord had not seen such soft hands on any carpenter he had every encountered, and so he watched and listened.

Whenever a servant from the big house came in for a libation, Mr Mosely (for so he was called) abandoned his other companions to join them, seeking to engage them in conversation. Only the under butler was at all loose in his tongue after Mosely offered some strong spirits, talking about his lordship freely. A word dropped into the servant's ear about the landlord's suspicions relating to the moleskin waistcoat made the man drink up and leave. During the day, Mr Mosely was absent, giving the landlord to believe that as a city dweller usually, Mr Mosely wished to take advantage of the wonderful countryside. As he had neither gun nor rod, he professed himself a lover of walking, though from his pallid complexion, the landlord doubted it. On the third day the big bluff landlord, Joe Shepherd, gave word to the tap boy, an intelligent lad of twelve years old, to follow Mr Mosely at a distance without being seen. This was sport to the boy and he arrived back a little after the guest to report on his task with glee.

Mr Mosely had entered the estate grounds of Gascoigne Manor (by dint of a crumbled piece of the surrounding wall) and walked around there all day, engaging the cottagers in conversation, asking questions about yields, gardens, stock, stables, as though he were some sort of agent of his lordship's. He took most interest in the inhabitants of the lodge (the landlord frowned at this) and asked some questions about the viscount.

The next day before breakfast, the little 'journeyman' had gone, leaving a generous amount with a chambermaid to cover his shot. He had departed on the London mail coach, and accompanying him, had he but known it, was a letter from the landlord - addressed to Gascoigne House in London - which had been left out the night before with some others, for the mail coach to add to its leather sack of correspondence.

#

Foster and Galbraith of the *League* seemed to resent it somewhat that Gascoigne did not ask for help with the wooing of Miss Delacroix. He wove his way even into the middle of the aunts that evening at Almacks club, leaving them nothing to do. He skilfully made some light remark to Lady Pelleter, who smiled in spite of herself, complimented Lady Eloise (still at the forefront of fashion) on her dress and even suggested a new milliner to Lady Sybilla.

'And just how, my lord Gascoigne, would you know so much of a fashionable lady's accoutrements?' asked Mrs Sybilla Lynfield sternly.

'Only for such moments as these, dear Mrs Lynfield, do I make it my business to know,' he said bowing over her hand and delivering her the full light of his roguish smile.

As he slid away to claim her niece's hand for a dance, she murmured to her sister Mags, 'He is just *too* fascinating.'

'Pshaw!' returned her sister, but she watched Gascoigne and Delphine together and sighed.

The dance was a waltz, which Miss Delacroix had only recently been permitted by the patronesses at Almacks to do. Heaven forfend that a young lady in her first season accepted an invitation to waltz without the gentleman being first presented to her by Lady Jersey, or Princess Esterhazy or one of the other powerful patronesses.

She had not waltzed with the viscount before and she was rather shy for a moment when his hand rested on her back.

'You were unwell, Miss Delacroix? I came over with my poor offering of a nosegay yesterday afternoon only to see it being added to a tray of them.'

'Yes, I received a great many flowers.' She said it flatly, and took a breath. 'I have to speak to you, sir-'

'Well first,' he said instructively, while whirling her round, 'you should thank me for the flowers, you know.'

'Thank you. Now-'

'Which were they?'

'I beg your pardon?'

'Which flowers?'

'Well, how should I know? I got a dozen such things,' she said crossly.

'Didn't you read the cards?'

'Yes I read them - but I cannot remember-'

'You should read the tender sentiments on each gentleman's card and then tell him that his choice was quite the prettiest of all. It is only polite. I met Mr Crawford at the door and he told me he had torn up five cards in his efforts to express his feelings.'

'Which flowers were his?'

'The violets, I believe.'

She frowned, 'But that card only said, "Give me a smile and you give me my delight."'

'You are supposed to read his meaning within. I venture to think that your smile this evening would let him know he was preferred.'

'Well, I am very glad I have not smiled. How absurd.'

'*His* card you remember. *Mine* you have forgotten,' he said tragically.

'Your flowers were roses and your card read, "I hope that you feel more yourself soon, G." I thought the G arrogant. As though I must recognise it. Am I supposed to find a hidden meaning in your card? Does it conceal an offer of marriage?' He laughed. 'And are we really going to talk all night about nosegays when I have something important to say to you?'

Gascoigne looked around him and with great aplomb spun Miss Delacroix out of the tall French doors that led to a terrace. They stopped moving and stood in the moonlight for a moment, gazing at each other. She moved back from his arms, which without the excuse of the dance seemed somehow suggestive. Looking around she spied a bench by the wall and sat, and in a very unusual, welcoming gesture, raised her hand to his to pull him beside her.

'Thank you,' she said simply. He opened his mouth and she could tell it was to make another jest. Her little glove hand stopped his mouth and he saw she was grave. 'And not for the flowers. For what you made me see of myself the last time we met. How cruelly I treated poor Miss Beauford and well, everyone really.'

A protest came from his throat.

'Did you know that my generous mama gave Mrs Beauford's widowed mother a cottage in our village not fit to live in - and called it charity? Did you know that my dear Phoebe is still grateful for the hovel? And did you know that while I have made some effort to improve her cottage, I *still* never thought to ask her how she found herself there? She grew up comfortably in a Manor house in Devon, but the property was entailed and her cousin threw her mama and two girls out without providing for them at all. And I never knew, till you showed me how wrong I was, how self-centred. It distressed me greatly. I did not know how I could bear it.'

'My dear girl,' Gascoigne said, grasping her gloved hands, 'do not distress yourself. I have no right, *none*, in berating someone for selfishness. That has been the entire sum of my life!'

Their eyes met in the darkness, they seemed to lean towards each other without volition, when a sharp voice said, 'Delphine! Are you still unwell? Perhaps tonight was too soon for you; I will take you home.'

They sprang apart like guilty children caught in the pantry, and Gascoigne bowed, saying, 'My Lady Pelleter!' then left the terrace.

Delphine rose and with some of her usual coldness, followed her aunt.

#

Mr Mosely and his moleskin waistcoat took a turn around Cribb's Parlour, where nobs, and Captain-Sharps and working gents like himself mixed freely, only supposing an interest in gin and the sporting life. Mr Mosely was enough of a player to move unmarked around the place, joining a variety of tables and getting the occupants into conversation with a volley of gin-soaked confidences. Had anyone been watching more than usual, they might have seen him hold his single gin without drinking, even though his voice slurred the more he talked. But this was only remarked upon by two beefy newcomers with cudgels in their pockets, who had scanned the room and given each other the nod, before leaving the warmth of the bar and melting back into the London mist.

#

A small package addressed in a spiky hand, arrived at Gascoigne House and Burton brought it to his master, who tossed it to one side as though burned. Two such others had come, the first and largest one he had seen opened by his Lordship, containing a large quantity of bills, some of which he had been set to distribute among the staff. His lordship had opened the bulging drawer of bills that made even the stalwart Burton shiver, and he had not to be disturbed for the next few hours - after which a collection of missives addressed to creditors had made a high pile on a silver salver, to be delivered around town by Rupert the first footman. The staff were happy to have their faith in their master restored once more, but Burton was uneasy. So his master was in funds again, but he had not mentioned to Burton, or to his man, a big win at the Faro Bank or elsewhere. So how had Lord Gascoigne come into this money? Perhaps Burton, whose discretion was gold standard, would not have been troubled but for the quantity of cognac the viscount had drunk in the hours when he did his business.

The next day, too, his man of business, Clayton, had visited and after some hours and mounds of paperwork, during which Burton had provided refreshments, the butler noted the diminution in the banknotes as well as the brandy bottle. His master was not in celebratory mood. Relieved, perhaps, but there was no celebration. Showing Mr Clayton out, Burton heard him assure the viscount that he would post to Shropshire forthwith, and that he would do as instructed when he reached the Manor house. My lord Gascoigne kept the brandy bottle company deep into the night, and Burton sensed that he was drowning his sorrows, or perhaps - and Burton didn't know how this was suggested to him - his shame.

Today's packet, in the same hand, was the double of another, smaller one that had been delivered a month since. It was soft, and Burton guessed that it held yet more banknotes. The viscount, however, on receiving it, looked foul. It joined its unopened mate on the mantle, silent and sinister.

The viscount hardly wanted to touch them.

#

Aunt Sybilla and Aunt Mags Pelleter had sought, on the carriage ride home from Almacks, to drum into Delphine the wrong she had done in leaving the ballroom with Lord Gascoigne, whilst her companion Miss Phoebe sat cowering in a corner. 'It was only that *I* was the one to notice, and mercifully no one else, which has saved your reputation, Delphine.'

Delphine stiffened, as was her wont, and then she seemed to shake it off. She replied to her aunt patiently, as though explaining to a child, 'But we were simply having a conversation, aunt. What is so shocking about that?'

'He was holding your hands, Delphine! And in public!'

Aunt Sybilla squeaked - although it may have been merely in response to the jostling of the coach on the cobbled streets.

'Should I only hold hands in private then?' Delphine asked, puzzled.

'You should not hold hands *at all*!' Lady Pelleter all but screamed. She sat back into the squabs, fanning herself and saying, 'You talk to her, Sybilla, for I cannot.'

Sybilla sat forward grasping her niece's hands once more, 'Delphine, you must listen to us, I do assure you. Your conduct tonight was shocking. Alone with a man, permitting him to take liberties, this can only lead to ruination in the eyes of the world. If one of the patronesses had seen you, you might have been labelled fast and denied vouchers to Almacks again.'

'But I assure you he was only comforting me as you are now, aunt. There was nothing shameful-'

Mags Pelleter sprang back upright as though she were a jack-in-the-box. 'I *saw* you Delphine - do not dare to tell me it wasn't an intimate moment-'

'Well, I suppose it was. But there was nothing sordid about it. It was just that I was telling Lord-'

'It does not matter,' nearly screamed her aunt, 'what you thought you were doing, Delphine. It is what men like Gascoigne have planned for just such innocents as you. If you had been seen - why, my Roberta and Eloise's Christiana would have been tainted by your shame-'

'Really?' said Delphine in wonder. 'But if girls cannot talk to men on their own, how do they ever get asked to marry?'

'Well,' said Mrs Lynfield confidentially, 'of course mamas will sometimes orchestrate a little alone time, of course. To bring the man to the point, so to speak-'

'*Sy-bill-a!*' screamed Lady Pelleter.

'Sorry, my dear!' said her sister contritely, 'I should say, Delphine, that the correct gentleman will ask the father of the lady if he can speak to her alone,' she said primly, 'but only so that he may ask her to marry him.'

Mags Pelleter threw herself back onto the squabs again, fanning herself, 'She refuses to understand Sybilla, I-'

'I am very sorry to distress you Aunt Mags, I will not do it again.'

The aunts looked at her, dumbfounded. Mags deflated like a stuck balloon. ‘Oh, heaven help us, she agrees. And I am *still* not convinced.’

CHAPTER 7

Miss Beauford came to Delphine's room that night, to see if she was upset by the events of the evening.

'My dear Delphine, are you quite well?'

Delphine was sitting in bed, hugging her legs, deep in thought.

'Phoebe! Pray come and sit with me. I'm sorry you had to suffer that carriage ride - are *you* quite alright?'

Miss Beauford hopped onto the bed, hitching her own legs up, facing the still Delphine. 'Quite alright my dear.'

'What age are you, dear Phoebe?'

'I am thirty eight years now. On my last short visit to London I was twenty one, and that was four years after my debut. I was presented to Queen Charlotte you know, before the king's sad illness. I was fortunate that my sister's court dress fitted me well, because though my papa was comfortably off, we were not rich.'

'How was it?' enquired Delphine.

'A little less exciting than I thought it would be, the queen merely nodded and I was passed over. However I did dance with a major-general, who admired my fine eyes.' Miss Beauford giggled and made Delphine smile.

'You still have very fine eyes.'

'I have been running on. How are you after your aunts - well, I was afraid you would become distressed again.'

'I distressed them, though I never meant to. I do think living in the world is difficult. I find it full of rules that I do not know I am breaking. It is assumed I will know them, but how can I? You of all people had a glimpse of my life with Mama. I think it never occurred to her that I would live outside Delacroix House, so only her rules mattered.'

'Can I ask - I would not dare, except that you refer to it - were you very unhappy, my dear?'

'Very. But I took respite in being angry. Not a hot anger that chafes at you. I had to quell that when I was very young. It was a cold anger that protected me from desiring more than I had.'

'Do you know, my dear, I think I was much richer than you all my life. For I had parents and a sister who loved me.'

'Phoebe, will you share my bed tonight? I am upset by I hardly know what and I do not wish to be alone.'

Miss Phoebe, delighted, pulled back a cover and slipped in beside her, quite naturally laying down her head and putting an arm round Delphine's waist, as she had used to do with her sister. Delphine stiffened, then relaxed, sliding down the sheets till she had her head on the pillow, the unexpected arm still about her, and slept as she had not slept since she arrived.

#

The aunts had determined that Delphine was to be under close guard for the moment, and the presence of Miss Phoebe Beauford was by no means enough.

'She is the sweetest woman in the world,' said Eloise, 'but her nature is not at all forceful and she cannot be depended on to keep Delphine out of a scrape.'

'I'd have thought the constant chaperonage was quite enough to do so, however silly the chaperone,' said Mr Lynfield, sitting at a distance by the fire, reading his journal.

The three ladies rolled their eyes in his direction and ignored him for the moment. 'We must consult our schedules and keep Delphine with us at all times. This morning, Christiana and I go to the silk warehouse, for there is no hoping that she has sufficient evening gowns for the season, for she does not. I will include Delphine.'

'Then you could meet us for luncheon at Rosetti's,' said Mrs Lynfield, 'and I will accompany her to the lending library and then we can come home to greet visitors. Let us hope that there is one among them who can divert her thoughts from Gascoigne. Mr Steel is one of her favourites and I shall insist she drive with him tomorrow morning. This evening is the concert and we need not worry, Gascoigne never appears there.'

'And you can make yourself useful, Edgar,' said Lady Pelleter to Mr Lynfield grimly, 'You can seek out Gascoigne and ask him what he means with your niece.'

'I will do nothing so ill-advised,' drawled Mr Lynfield, without looking up from his journal.

'My dearest-,' said his wife in a pleading voice.

'It is of no use trying to persuade me. If I were to ask him what he wants with my niece, then if he is the man you suspect him of being and he means her a mischief he will hardly tell me so. And if he says that he wishes to marry her like an honest man, what can I say to that?'

'That you forbid it!' cried the redoubtable Mags.

'Forbid a peer of the realm from offering his hand and heart and privileges to a commoner?'

'But he is a fortune hunter!'

'Then perhaps he has found his fortune.'

'And he is a libertine and a gambler and-'

'Everything silly young girls find irresistible, I know.'

'You would see your niece sell herself into a life such as that-'

'Cannot you ladies see,' uttered Mr Lynfield in goaded accents, 'That offering Delphine another sort of prison than she has already endured will only make her throw off the bonds and make Gascoigne more interesting?'

'We cannot leave things as they are - people are beginning to talk.'

'Yes, of Gascoigne's wooing of a debutante, not of anything untoward. I have observed them narrowly and Delphine does not exhibit any of the signs of infatuation. You should trust her - for she has a more sensible head than many. If I did not know better, I would think it was she using him, not the other way around.'

'Edgar!' said Lady Pelleter in the voice that made her husband quake, 'You will talk to Gascoigne!'

'No!' said Mr Lynfield, crossing his legs and snapping his paper in finality.

#

Christiana Carswell, a handsome girl with her mothers' light hair and elegant figure, was not quite happy that her cousin accompany them, for she had lately been ignored by a young man of fashion, Mr Mark Steel, who had spent the start of the season in her pocket, as the crude would have it, only to be led away by the bright star of her cousin. That he had to wait in line to dance with Delphine, and that she showed him no particular favour, made her resent her cousin more, not less. Delphine had not had to lift a finger to steal her beau, and that she did not even realise it made no odds. But Christiana was a well behaved and good-natured girl and sharing the excitement of the silk warehouse soon made them friends.

Delphine had unerring eye for colour, it seemed, and though her manner of delivering her opinion left a lot to be desired, Christiana soon trusted her, 'I thought you might suit the yellow, with your beautiful hair, but it makes you look sallow-' said the cousin as Christiana held it under her chin. 'The rose is perfect!'

This beautiful pink silk had hundreds of tiny rosebuds already embroidered upon it, and Lady Eloise looked at the tag only to move her daughter along. It was by far too expensive. A brief word with the warehouse satellite who was following them suggested Delphine was purchasing it for herself. The ladies found also some day-muslins and some silk mousseline, not too dear, and bought lengths, Delphine ordering one of the plainest, that Miss Phoebe had admired, to be sent to Russell Square. They found a primrose that became Christiana, some heavenly blues and turquoise for Delphine and were presently comfortably sated and happy to go to luncheon.

During this meal, Delphine announced her intention of visiting the lending library this afternoon, but to be back in time for the 'at home' of her aunt Sybilla. 'Oh, I shall accompany you there today, my dear Delphine, for I have not changed my book in an age.'

Delphine exchanged a look with Miss Phoebe, for only she knew that after a whirling visit to the library, Delphine met with her man of business on Thursday afternoons. Miss Phoebe usually sat in the outer office with a young man on a high perch stool and desk, who often nipped down to buy her refreshments from the street vendors who called and whom she eventually enjoyed chatting to, as he went about his not too taxing tasks. Miss Phoebe had seen no harm in this, for Delphine had explained their old friendship and that she wished to know a little more of her inheritance. Delphine may be unchaperoned, but anyone seeing the advanced decrepitude of Mr Rigby-Blythe could hardly be concerned. But silence reigned about these visits and Miss Phoebe realised, with a start of guilt, that they had been kept secret.

When her aunts had risen to go and refresh herself between courses, Delphine rose and took up her gloves and reticule. 'Pray tell my aunts that I have some business in town that I forgot and will be sure to return for the 'at home' today. Come Phoebe.'

Christiana had hardly had time to do more than mumble before Delphine and Phoebe were in the street and hailed a taxi.

The girl was gently scolded by her mama, but had forgiven her cousin by later that afternoon, when the silk draper's wares had arrived and they included several yards of the rose silk, with a few words of Delphine's attached begging her cousin to accept it and to send a length of gold satin she had chosen for her darker cousin Roberta. It was a gift of friendship, Delphine had added, and as Christiana, showed her mother, that dame sighed and admitted that it was very prettily done.

Mrs Lynfield had arrived home in a rage, and would have taken Delphine to task, but when her husband arrived shortly - after Delphine who was now changing her dress - he said that Gascoigne had spent all day in the club, so her worst fears were assuaged.

Where, then, did she go? Mrs Lynfield trapped Miss Phoebe, who told her. This news she took to her husband in his chamber and she wrested with his cravat as she complained. 'Let her have her friendship with her man of business - for what harm can it do?' he told her calmly, his chin lifted so that she could work on the knot of the cravat that he sought to change, 'He's already agreed to run everything through me before he acts, but I think Delphine sees him as more of a grandfather figure in her life. Leave her alone, my love. She was watched and spied upon all her life, she probably needs a few secrets to feel her new freedom.'

Mrs Lynfield, soft at heart, was much struck by that. She had promised to allow her niece to have some joy in London, to be free of all that her cold mother did to her, but now she and all the sisters were behaving exactly like Emilia - a thought that chilled her to the bone. But there was still the problem of Gascoigne.

She would have to deal with the viscount herself.

#

'The B M at four!' said the missive, hand-delivered to Gascoigne by a sweeping boy who was now chinking his greatest ever *largesse* in his threadbare pockets, for the lady had given him a florin for delivering and the gentleman a quarter sovereign for accepting. 'It must be some billy-doo for that!' said his friend, 'Arry.

The viscount had scratched his head a little whilst reading the ode to brevity, guessing that the aunts had forced her to feel herself "*in extremis*" and that she wanted him to make a bolt for the British Museum.

Whatever his reputation, he did not have a taste for the clandestine, so he bowled up to Russell Square in his tilbury, and knocked politely on the door of Mr Lynfield's abode at three o'clock. Using the ease of rank and previous connection to the family, he handed his hat and crop lazily to the footman and asked if the ladies were at home.

Fiennes, the butler, who had heard enough of the sisters' conversation to understand that Lord Gascoigne might not, at the moment, be welcome, walked forward.

'Mrs Lynfield is not at home, my lord,' he said discreetly, 'perhaps your lordship will return tomorrow when you will be sure to find her.' He had taken the hat and crop from James as he spoke and he offered them deferentially to the viscount.

The viscount, with laughing eyes, dropped his voice conspiratorially and said, with what Fiennes considered an insinuating manner, 'Ah, but it is not Mrs Lynfield I seek. Miss Delacroix has requested me by letter to take her and her companion to the British Museum this afternoon and you see me all eagerness to oblige.'

The butler was caught. This was not, he was sure, what his mistress would wish, and yet with neither master nor mistress present and no orders to the contrary, who was he to gainsay a Viscount?

'I shall enquire of Miss Delacroix whether she will see you.'

Ten minutes later, a hurried Miss Delacroix in a green carriage dress with a white spencer atop came rapidly down the stairs, followed by her companion, who was still tying the strings of her simple straw bonnet. Miss Delacroix shot him a look that bode ill for him later, and walked past him to the door. The footman opened it and it was but a moment before the cool Miss Delacroix and party were bowling through the London streets and she was able to turn a furious gaze on the viscount.

'What on earth did you mean by it, coming to the house?'

'Why, *you* wished for this expedition to the dullest place in London, and I am obliging you. Even driving you the three streets distance to save your pretty slippers.'

'You knew that I wished to go in secret, for I explained it all to you.'

'And *I* did not. We are bound to meet someone there we know, and how would it look if your aunts were ignorant of it? I have no taste for that sort of intrigue.'

'By your reputation, my lord, you have a taste for all sorts of intrigue,' said Delphine pertly.

'Oh, but never with single ladies,' said the outrageous viscount.

Since they had had to check the horses behind a cart, Miss Phoebe could hear this last exchanged and choked.

'You are-'

'Despicable, licentious, wicked-' said Gascoigne, bored, 'Pick one.'

'Very obliging to take me to the museum,' said Delphine in a saintly tone. 'I just needed to say something particular to you, and since I could not seem to commit it to paper, I judged it better to see you.'

'Well, said his lordship, negotiating an overbalanced cart, 'if you have something particular to say, you had best leave it till the British Museum. It'll give us something to do besides boring ourselves to death.'

Delphine looked at the streets, turning over her handkerchief as she did so. She did not speak again, except to say. 'I did not summon you to fight with you.'

He turned his fox eyes on her and delivered her a warm and intimate smile, which made Miss Phoebe, who could only see it in profile, wonder what devastating effect it would have on her cousin when she looked at it full on. Delphine looked away however, and soon they arrived at the British Museum. She had known from her reading in childhood that admission was free to all 'studious and curious persons', but this party hardly qualified.

After wandering rather aimlessly around the rooms, the viscount spied a bench in a room ascribed to Lord Elgin's collection of classical sculpture, and led the ladies to it. It was difficult to drag her eyes away from the exquisite marble figures, but Delphine had a task to finish. She turned to Miss Phoebe, holding out her hand. 'Phoebe dear, please will you be seated on the bench in the corner? I have a need to say something privately to Lord Gascoigne. I promise it is nothing that my aunts would disapprove of.'

Miss Phoebe was very sure that this whole expedition was something her aunts would disapprove of, but she could not resist that pleading look, or the accompanying smile from this girl who had given so much to her in so short a time. She turned to Lord Gascoigne and gave him an unaccustomed frown. He took her hand and said, most solemnly, 'I shall not play Miss Delacroix false, I do assure you.'

Gascoigne began, once they were alone, 'Your aunts have given you a tearing row about Almacks,' he said, 'I'm sorry. Completely my fault.'

'They believe you had ill plans for me.'

'At Almacks? I wouldn't dare. Lady Jersey was a friend of my mother's - she'd flay me alive.'

'Well I know you meant no harm, it was *I* who wished to speak-'

'I would not say *no* harm precisely-' he said ruefully.

There was a frisson that passed through Delphine's body when she remembered their leaning towards each other. 'Something happened between us,' she said honestly, 'which, whatever my aunts say, I do not believe was planned.'

She looked up at him inquiringly, and he wondered for a moment if anyone had ever been kissed in the British Museum's Antiquities Hall. 'No, not planned.'

'But it makes what they say of us truer than not, you see. It would be very easy to-' she stopped herself and he would have given anything to understand what she had been about to say. 'I chose you to do something for me. You have been most helpful. You have corrected my tongue, reviewed my suitors, and been truly honest with me in all your dealings, I believe. If your teasing ways also make me angry, that is was my deserts for choosing a man such as you.'

'A man such as me,' he said coldly, 'you seem to be making a summation, Miss Delacroix.'

'Have I hurt you? I seem to do that easily to the people closest to me without meaning to.' He said nothing. 'I wanted to say that I seem to be hurting my aunts in ways they do not deserve. Going onto the terrace with you could even, my Aunt Mags told me, have affected the reputation of my cousins, had we been discovered.' Gascoigne thought this an hysterical exaggeration, but said nothing. 'You have done your best for me, my Lord Gascoigne, but now I must manage on my own.' Gascoigne gave her a look that seemed to have closed off and show that he was very far from her, though they were seated so close. 'I shall not drive with you, or even dance with you anymore. Our arrangement still stands, if I become engaged before the end of the season, I shall gift the five thousand pounds. You will have earned it, for you have steered me past the worst of them all.'

'Excepting myself.' He said from that far-off place.

'Excepting only that,' he thought he heard her mutter.

'Your appraisal of me as a suitor has not changed, then? I see. Well, I shall have the attendant hail you a hackney, my dear.' He took the hand she offered and bowed over it. 'Goodbye, Miss Delacroix, I hope for you all you wish for yourself.' He turned and was gone, too stone of face to even acknowledge Miss Phoebe as he passed her.

Delphine put her head in her hands and wept, Miss Phoebe running to her side, and gathering her in her arms and rocking her, warning an attendant away with the sternest of glances that she was capable of.

CHAPTER 8

'Delphine!' screeched her Aunt Sybilla as she entered the green room, still wearing her bonnet and gloves, 'What do you mean by it, going off with -'

'We shall not be seeing any more of Lord Gascoigne, aunt,' her niece said, in a voice as cold as the grave. 'You may let your sisters know that our - friendship - is quite at an end.'

Behind her cold look, thought Sybilla Lynfield, was a desolate look that shook her aunt to her core.

#

A meeting of *The Wed or Dead League* in the last week had seen The Honourable Daniel Galbraith claim Miss Frampton as his target (declaring her nose to be a handsome match for his own) and therefore Gascoigne, who would rather have left town for his hunting lodge in Suffolk, was honour bound to attend the soirée at Lady Glendale's.

As Lady Glendale was a bluestocking, the entertainment for the evening was poetry, so only the oaths that Lockhart, Foster, Gascoigne, de Chabernet (for he was in town) and Deville had sworn to the League, would have brought them within a mile of the place.

'Foggy says his mother told him that you took Miss Delacroix to the *British Museum*!' whispered Hildegard incredulously, as Lord Enderly, that elderly roué, finally finished his ode to his hostess.

'Foggy, for once, was correct,' said Gascoigne shortly, alerted by a stir at the door - Miss Delacroix's arrival. Mr Mark Steel, open and charming, led her and her companions (Miss Phoebe and Lady Carswell) to chairs on the opposite wall. Miss Delacroix's eyes scanned the room and passed over the *League* members with no form of recognition.

'She blanked you!' said Hildegard, hissing.

'Ssh!' said Gascoigne briefly, 'our hostess commences to read.'

Miss Frampton also entered, closely followed by her parents, who took place on either side of her.

'Difficult,' said Hildegard regarding the straight-laced parents, 'Very difficult.'

The Honourable Daniel sighed, but Lockhart leaned his great body across, 'Nothing easier for *The Wed or Dead League*, boy.'

Lord Lockhart moved across to the Frampton party and leaned over the father's chair, whispering something. Mr Frampton rose, with every sign of relief, and followed Lockhart quietly, so as not to disturb their hostess in full flight of verse.

'The promise of better refreshment than the ratafia,' said Gascoigne admiringly, 'it never fails.'

'As long as he can find some in this god-forsaken house,' murmured the Marquis.

'But the mother!' sighed Galbraith.

'I'll take care of that!' said Foster, laughing.

They watched as Hildegard, armed only with his punch, wandered in the direction of the Framptons, and somehow managed to spill the red liquid over the costly silk of Mrs Frampton's dress.

'Ruthless!' muttered Gascoigne, shaking his head.

The lady rose and Hildy led her apologetically to the door, hopeful of finding a maid to help remove the punch before the dress was quite spoilt.

Daniel Galbraith was seated beside Miss Frampton in a trice, and another gentleman who had admired her, the handsome Mr Sinclair, was going to attend her too, when Gascoigne intercepted him and asked him to join his friends, putting a flattering arm about his shoulders. It was a full twenty minutes before the parents returned, and by that time the red-haired lover had arranged a meeting time with his love, giving her to understand that if she would not meet him, he may as well shoot himself. Tender-hearted Miss Frampton was not inclined to let him suffer such a fate, and Gascoigne felt that the business was nearly all done. It was only a decision between a runaway match (Miss Frampton was just eighteen) and a hysterical demand to her parents.

Two days later, when the League had attended an Almacks assembly and a concert at Vauxhall Gardens, ("Devilish dull", opined the miserable Deville) helping Daniel Galbraith to finish the job, the gentlemen all met once more at Cribb's Parlour.

The Marquis raised his glass to the newly engaged gentlemen, who had convinced the daughter, then the father, of his desire to turn over a new leaf. 'A job well done, gentlemen. To *The Wed or Dead League*, soon to be no more.'

Hildegard Foster stood, holding his glass in toast. 'I make a claim, gentlemen!'

'Ha!' cried the Marquis, raising his too, 'Our very last claimant! An *historique* occasion!'

'Not quite the last, I fear,' said Hildegard Foster, with brio, 'I claim Miss Delphine Delacroix.'

The viscount's tankard hit the table hard enough to split it. There was a tense silence.

'That lady has been claimed already my boy,' said Lord Lockhart warningly.

'She has,' said Hildegard, trying to hold the eye of Gascoigne and failing. 'But you gentlemen have attended the same events this week as I. It is perfectly obvious the viscount has - eh - failed in his endeavour. Miss Delacroix as near as cut him dead. Everyone is talking of it.' Every man looked at Gascoigne, who clenched his jaw. 'So given our rules, Miss Delacroix is once more available to be claimed.'

'Not by you, you scoundrel,' the viscount hissed.

'Gentlemen, by the rules of our League, you must support me,' said Hildegard doggedly, a mulish look to his mouth.

The viscount stood. 'I tell you now, and you had better believe me, Foster. Miss Delacroix is not available to you or anyone else in this League. And if you attempt to do more than dance with her I swear to you that I will flay you to death like the cur you are.'

His gloves were in his hand and he slapped them across Foster's flushed face. He turned and left the room.

'Ah, it is a love match, I think,' said the Marquis solemnly.

'Then you won't help me?' Hildegard said, his flushed countenance betraying his fury. The other men looked at him, silent. 'Well, I will help myself.' And he too, left Cribb's dramatically.

Captain Fanshaw Redmond followed. He had not heard the conversation, but he knew when a young man was vulnerable, and when to take his chance.

#

Over the next few weeks, the *ton* watched in fascination as Miss Delacroix, whom all the world accepted as an entertaining eccentric, dealt with her court. Precisely what had happened to her favourite, Viscount Gascoigne, was unknown. He had disappeared to his hunting lodge for two weeks and when he came back it was to find his friend, Hildegard Foster, paying court to Miss Delacroix.

There appeared to be any number still in the running, Foster, Mark Steel and Sir Roger Fentiman among them; and there was an entry in the betting book at one gentleman's club listing all the runners and more, including Lord Gascoigne.

'Thought he was out of the running,' said Lord Alvanley, 'I hear she doesn't even look his way.'

'A falling out, certainly, but there are still good odds on him. It would help to know who fell out with whom, but he's a closed trap on the subject. But watch for the dark horse, I say!'

Alvanley put five hundred on Steel, then scratched it and put it on the viscount. 'Never to be discounted, Titus!'

Miss Delacroix was herself thinning the field. She excused herself from dancing with Sir Reid Cameron, whose eyes followed her around the room in what even her aunts came to admit was a most uncomfortable way. And there was many a story of the sharp edge of her tongue - given to gentlemen who she felt took liberties. One story was that when Captain Fanshaw Redmond, a suave womanizer of the old school, had wondered if she would like him to take her into supper she said that she could think of nothing she would like less.

She seemed to have made friends with her cousins, The Honourable Miss Christiana Carswell and the dark sprite Lady Roberta Pelleter and if gentlemen approached them as they congregated to gossip, Miss Delacroix waved them off with that imperious hand. In a miracle, felt by some to be close to Moses parting the Red Sea, she got Foggy Carswell to talk to a woman normally. At least once at every party they attended where Foggy had been compelled by his Mama to accompany her and his sister, he and Miss Delacroix danced and were seen to talk and even laugh. When asked what they spoke of, Foggy was vague. ‘Lord, I don’t know. She’s a dashed entertaining girl.’

The gentlemen of the *ton* watched in awe whilst Miss Delacroix introduced the Honourable Mr Carswell to young ladies of her acquaintance, then sit patiently while he tried to converse with them. Everyone knew Foggy could never speak to women of his own class under forty without his trademark flush and bobbing Adam’s apple. His sport, they knew, was with a different class of woman altogether. But they looked on as Miss Delacroix soothed his way with the debutantes, and soon he was encouraged to ask girls to dance without stuttering or blushing even once.

They watched as even his mama Lady Carswell, regarding this last with bated breath, was amazed. She had to beg a handkerchief from her formidable sister Lady Pelleter, whose fierce eyes were also a little moist.

It was noted too, that gentlemen who first danced with her companion Miss Beauford, the plain poor relation of whom she was inordinately fond, would not afterwards be refused by Miss Delacroix. This ensured that for a spinster of a certain age, Miss Beauford danced as frequently as a town belle.

Gascoigne's arrival at Lady Selkirk's ball was treated by most of the room as the beginning of a sporting attraction. Miss Delacroix and he managed to dance all night without ever being in the same set. The viscount was charming and engaging. He danced with old friends and new ones, and gave no less than three debutantes the benefit of his charming smile. No one could find that they glanced each other's way, but Gascoigne betrayed himself with a darkling look at his friend, the handsome Hildegard Foster, just after he had led Miss Delacroix off the floor.

'You have to be deuced aware of each other,' said the wise old Duke of Bromley, 'to keep so far apart as that all night.' Of those who heard this, three gentlemen put money down on Gascoigne, the long shot.

#

Gascoigne, inclined at first to empty the cognac bottle and go to the devil after Delphine had sent him off, had decided on a different course of action. He spent the next morning in earnest conversation with Clayton, his man of business and Burton was pleased to see that the cognac was barely touched and that the viscount emerged with a new, if rather frenetic, energy. He departed for his hunting lodge after he had kept some pressing, he said, engagements. As one of these was Lady Glendale's poetry evening, Burton could not help wonder if Miss Delacroix was somehow behind it. All the household knew about Miss Delacroix, of course. The groom had let interesting titbits drop to his lordship's valet, the whole world knew she was the latest heiress, and everyone hoped the romance would prosper. But the viscount did not return from these latest social occasions happy, but at least he did not again assault the cognac bottle.

He returned from his hunting box in Suffolk to find his mail laid out on a platter on his desk. In amongst the gilt-edged invitations and some business correspondence, he spied a small soft package, written in a spiky hand.

'By all that's holy, Burton, what is this?' he picked the package up and dropped it once more as though it had been a hot coal.

'It came for you on Thursday sir, a month to the day when the last arrived.'

The viscount felt along the tall mantle for the other two packets, and dropped them on to the desk with the third. 'Give me five minutes, and then I want James to take this directly to an address I shall give him in the city.

He sat at a table and wrote,

Mr Rigby-Blythe,

My business arrangement with Miss Delacroix being at an end, I enclose the monthly payments. In the next weeks I should be able to return to you the funds already advanced, and that should be an end to it.

Your servant, sir,
Gascoigne.

He took the large sheet of vellum and wrapped it around the three small packages, then sealed it with his own seal, and scribbled an address on the front. 'Burton,' he cried, moving into the hall, 'Get rid of that now.'

Burton, catching sight of the package in his hands, looked at the viscount's blazing eyes and did not consider the cognac bottle safe tonight.

#

Mr Rigby-Blythe had decided to wait until their weekly appointment to tell Miss Delacroix about the package. She did not take it well.

'Unopened, you say?' she demanded.

'All three.'

'Let me see that!' She read the note avidly and said indignantly, 'What does he mean by it? Our terms were quite clear. He failed to use the monthly stipend and now he wishes to pay back the advance? How *can* he without quite ruining himself - and for what?'

Mr Rigby-Blythe merely looked at her from beneath his caterpillar eyebrows, and ventured nothing in reply. She began pacing the room. 'What am I to do now?' she asked. 'I have received his services and now he will not accept payment and he is going to do something ridiculous to try to find the rest. We must stop him!'

Mr Blythe said nothing.

'Don't you see - he will be ruined!'

'No more than he was before he met you, my child. Lord Gascoigne's debts were not of your making.'

'Nor of his, I believe. He inherited them.'

'So I understand, if my information is correct, Lord Gascoigne has reduced his debts, paying off many of his father's creditors. But he is still very much encumbered.'

'We must, at least, make him accept the original sum.'

'I think the letter shows his determination not to do so.'

'*I* have done this. I have made it worse for him, just as he has made everything better for me. He *must* accept it. It is his pride - because I cut him off. I am so clumsy. Phoebe said that we should have remained friends - that I was too harsh - and Foggy Carswell says that the whole world is talking about it, how I have dropped him. I've humiliated him - I did not think how the world would view it - and now, because of his pride I will ruin him.'

'Why, my dear child, if you were not angry with him, did you "drop him" as you called it? Why not be friends?'

'It is not possible for me to be only friends with Lord Gascoigne.'

'Well,' said the old attorney gently, 'he is the stuff of story book heroes. Every young girl's dream.'

'I don't know that, I was never allowed story books of that description. I picked him because he was exactly what I didn't want and thus he was no threat. When I began to find that he was exactly what I do want, it was too late.'

'Then why do you not let yourself fall, my dear?'

'Because he is still all those other things, and I am not mad. I want a stable, sensible man - not someone who throws his hat into the ring for my fortune-'

'He does not seem to want your fortune now. Not any part of it.'

Delphine stopped dead. 'Do you think this is a trick? Like dancing with my friend so as to not seem too interested?'

Mr Rigby-Blythe shrugged. 'You know him better, do *you*?'

'No.' she sat on the chair again and cried.

He looked down fondly at her blond head. For the Snow Queen, an appellation he had heard that the Beau Monde bestowed on her, she had melted fast.

He opened the office door. 'Miss Phoebe, will you come in, please?'

#

Without the backing of *The Wed or Dead League,* Mr Hildegard Foster did not feel himself to be making sufficient progress. His case was desperate. He might lose his lodgings within the month if his shot wasn't paid, he was being dunned constantly, and a large sum he had borrowed from a friend to put on a horse had been lost when the nag (who'd been tipped to win by a knowing 'un in Cribb's) wasn't placed. Payment of this debt was crucial - an unpaid gambling debt gave a man an unrecoverable reputation. He'd end his days abroad like poor Barney Fredricks, reduced to selling his coat for gin.

He was truly scared. Miss Delacroix was the answer. Only be engaged to her and his friend would discreetly wait for the debt to be paid without spilling the beans; his tailor would make his groom clothes without a blink; and his landlord would roll out a red carpet. But getting close to Miss Delacroix was not as easy as Gascoigne had made it look.

He had enjoyed three dances and one carriage ride with Delphine and her dratted companion and had found none of these equal to a real flirtation. He had complimented the silver glint to her hair in what he thought of some of his best lines, but Delphine had merely said, 'So I have heard, sir.' And changed the subject. Her eyes were totally enthralling and he found being near her had started a fire in him that stopped his natural ability for light chatter. To have her in his arms for the one waltz was intoxicating, and he was getting desperate for more than Miss Delacroix's fortune. He was at a loss of how to proceed, afraid of Gascoigne's looks and bereft of his league's support, turned to his new friend.

'If you could just get her companion off of me Fanshaw, that would mean I could propose in the Park.'

Fanshaw grinned and filled up his gin glass once more. 'I could do that, my boy, quite easily, but would it be enough to ensure the readies? From what you say, you're in the suds deep and to get you out might prove harder than you think.'

'I've got to give it a shot-'

'I know, boy, I know. But what are the chances she'll say yes? Short odds in the club are on Mark Steel.'

'That lightweight? - I have more address than him!' protested Foster slurring his words.

'Indeed you do. But it's not who is skilful so much as what style Miss Delacroix prefers. And she seems to prefer Steel's serious humour at the moment.'

'I swear I'd make her a good husband-' said Foster gloomily.

The Captain was keeping his glass well-filled. 'Of course you would my boy. And you wouldn't forget your friends either. You're a good chap.'

'I am. Not a cur, even if Gascoigne-'

'No, no my dear boy. But we may need to do a little something more drastic to show Miss Delacroix where her real interests lie. Something in the next few days would be best for you, I think - or the games up.'

'*You* mean like those old Irish chaps- ? Kidnap her and destroy her honour so that she has to marry-' he laughed derisively.

'You've got an idea there son. So, how are we going to do it?'

'You'll help me? You're a good fellow Fanshaw, best fellow in the world-'

As the boy's face hit the table, Fanshaw realised that he might have been too liberal with the spirits. He called for some paper and a quill, however, and began to scratch down ideas concerning the proposed abduction of Delphine Delacroix, the stuck-up princess whose icy tongue had caused him untold embarrassment.

CHAPTER 9

'I'm very sorry to interrupt you, my lord, but there is a gentleman of the legal profession awaiting you in the hall.'

'Mr Carter?'

'No, indeed my lord. A much different creature. A Mr Rigby-Blythe.'

'I have no more dealings with-! Oh, let him come in, Burton.'

'I will my lord, and bring a paregoric draught - the gentleman looks close to death.'

'Don't be concerned. He always looks like that. Just some tea and bread and butter will suffice.'

Burton sniffed with a "Don't say I didn't warn you" look, and went to let the lawyer in.

The viscount stood behind his large wooden desk, evidently regarding a paper of some import. Mr Rigby-Blythe waited patiently: these sort of games were not new to him. 'I thought we were all but finished our business Mr Rigby-Blythe?' the viscount drawled without looking up.

'I'm here at the behest of my client, sir,' said the attorney in his most apologetic tone. 'She is most anxious that you take back the six hundred pounds I sent to you.'

'You may tell her I will not.'

'I supposed so, that's why I have not brought the bills with me.'

The viscount looked up. 'Then why have you come, sir?'

'My client, Miss Delacroix, is most upset my lord-,' said the old man carefully, a fit of coughing suddenly gripping him as he saw his dismissal in the viscount's eyes.

The viscount moved forward. 'I beg your pardon sir, you are ill, please take a chair.'

Mr Rigby-Blythe did so, accepting the young man's help, his coughing stopping abruptly.

'Her concern, sir, I must say her passionate concern, is that in attempting to pay back the principal, you will ruin yourself.'

'That is no-one's business but my own,' said his lordship abruptly, throwing a suspicious look at the miraculously recovered lawyer.

'I tried to tell her so, my lord, but Miss Delacroix is a lady unlike any I have known. As cold and detached as she could be in her previous existence (and I always knew it to be only her defense) she can be as passionate and emotional now. This she attributes to you. You showed her the error of her ways, she feels, allowed her to see that she injured others when she failed to respond to their friendship.'

'That is absurd. A girl with such a heart as Miss Delacroix would have come to the realisation on her own.'

'Nevertheless, she said, and I believe her my lord, that she could not bear to be the cause of your ruination - and begs you will at least accept the principal.'

The viscount went back behind his desk and sat down. 'She is not the cause, they existed long before.'

'So I told her, my lord, but I am afraid that if you try to undo the good you have done yourself with her money, she will blame herself. Miss Delacroix in a passion is an untried entity - I do not know what she might do.'

'You put me in a difficult situation. I have no wish that my business be known.' Mr Blythe nodded. The viscount continued rather moodily, '-but if she is to make herself ill over it-. The truth is, taking the money never sat well with me. And Miss Delacroix's ending of our friendship spurred me on to try something I would have tried before, had I not been so set in my old resentments to think of it. I have broken the entail.'

'Broken the entail to a Gascoigne Manor? - it cannot have been done!' said Mr Rigby-Blythe with business-like certitude.

'No of course not! I can sell neither the Manor nor this house, nor any of my land, and I would not wish to. It is not my right, I am only a steward for my son, if I ever have one. No. My lawyer managed to break the entail to two other properties that were included - a hunting box in Suffolk and some land adjacent to it. My father kept that in order, at any rate, so it will yield a good price. The neighbour wants to buy it and there are two farms in the country that I can sell too.'

'But how was it managed?' said the old lawyer with professional curiosity. 'Oh, I beg pardon, your lordship - I have no right-'

'My man explained it to me thus, but I have no real grasp of the details. My father sold out funds, which were not entailed, and which he used to purchase the hunting box. His lawyer then went onto include this and the farmland into the entail, apparently to save it all being mortgaged by my ruinous papa, and it was done quickly and deliberately ill, my man Clayton thinks. Apparently old lawyer Jessup was fond of me and was quite capable of it. He disapproved of my father's excesses and my grandfather had made him promise to do what he could to save the inheritance from his dissolute son. He's dead now, so we may not verify that speculation.'

'Why would your papa have agreed to extend the entail? It was not in his interest.'

'My man Clayton suspects that lawyer Jessup may have had some grounds to blackmail him. Knowing Papa, that does not seem inconceivable. Old Jessup thus extended the entail with my interests in mind, but left, as it were a backdoor that I might break it. So Clayton believes. He had shown me previously that before the right judge the lock might be possible to break. I was sure it was a lost cause and I did not wish the humiliation of failing, so I did not pursue it. But now-'

'May I tell Miss Delacroix this?'

'No. Only enough to assure her that I am not about to go to the devil.'

'You can rely on me,' said Mr Rigby-Blythe, rising. He took the viscount's proffered hand once more. 'It seems to me,' he remarked sagely, 'that you and Miss Delacroix have had a beneficial effect one upon the other.'

'She does not think so,' said the viscount, once more immersed in his papers as the old man left.

#

Mr Hildegard Foster woke up with fuzzy head, limbs and mouth, on an unknown sofa. This was not unusual, so he merely groaned and looked about him, seeing what he expected, a small sitting room in what were obviously a neat set of gentleman's chambers. He scratched his fair head and sat up, addressing a small maid who was putting some coal on a fire, 'Where am I?' he said.

'Why, in Captain Redmond's chambers, my lord.'

Hildegard had the vaguest memory of some gin and chatter and so he said, somewhat relieved, 'Where is the Captain now?'

'Captain Redmond is dressing sir, in the bedroom. I am just going to bring the breakfast he ordered, sir.' She scuttled away and Hildegard sat with his head in his hands, to stop it rolling away, until the gallant captain emerged from his room.

'What-ho, Foster, is your head banging?'

'Just a trifle, Fanshaw. I do not think I could eat a bite,' remarked Foster, as the valet set the chairs and the maid brought in the breakfast dishes.

'Nonsense boy, in the Hussars we were known to hit the grog all night, have a solid feast of breakfast and be ready to fight the French before nine.'

They took seats around the table, and Hildegard accepted a roll, which he ate desultorily, but feeling better enough to take some slices of ham, some coddled eggs, a dish of mushrooms and some tea. Redmond regarded him with a benign eye, himself as cheery as if his only libation of last evening had been lemonade.

At last he lifted the paper upon which he had scratched the previous evening, saying, 'I think I have it all-.'

'All what?' said Hildegard, not particularly interested.

'Why all of your various plans for abducting Miss Delacroix.'

'No. I did not-'

'Well, you were past being able to write, of course. But you bade me write it all down and I have done, as you see.'

'I could not have-. I do remember mentioning it, but I would not really-'

'You are not alone my boy, I am pledged to aid you, you know.'

'I could not - it would be the work of a dastard.'

'If you did not mean to marry her, certainly. I could not consent to such a heinous plot if it were not for a good cause,' the captain said comfortably. 'Think now, Foster. She obviously likes you. And who other of her suitors would you prefer to yourself? Mark Steel? Once his fortune is discounted (for how can such a thing matter in the face of hers?) he has no more charms than you. Her head has been turned by so much male attention that it is impossible for her to make a decision, so we will make it for her.'

'No - Gascoigne!'

'He's threatened you - you said so last night. But once you are married the thing would be over.'

'Not *that*!' said Hildegard disgustedly. 'I don't *fear* him, but I feel that there is something between him and Miss Delacroix. It was only my desperation that made me think other. My friends tried to warn me-'

'Which friends?'

'The League-' said Foster, then held his tongue. 'It doesn't matter - they were right. I see it now.'

'They may be right as regards to Gascoigne, I cannot say. I have not remarked him wearing his heart on his sleeve. But they cannot be right about Miss Delacroix. Depend upon it, the viscount has done something to give her a disgust of him. She cannot bear to look his way, even.'

Foster shook his head, trying to ward off the alcohol's dark cloud. 'It may be so. But I could never abduct a lady - it was simply drunken ranting.'

'Think, Hildegard, what awaits you at home, what awaits you when your friend tells the world that you have reneged on a debt of honour. All you planned to do last night was to save Miss Delacroix from herself - and afterwards make her a wonderful husband. What is wrong in any of that?'

'I don't know - you're confusing me-,' uttered Hildegard. 'I suppose-'

This chink in the armour was all that Redmond needed. 'Let us go over the plans my boy. The best one was laid for tomorrow, I believe, whilst the ladies are walking in Hyde Park -'

'What's in this for you, Redmond?' demanded Foster when his head had cleared a little. 'You seem dashed eager to help me.'

'I cannot lie to you my boy. I often land in the suds myself, a Captain's pension not being what it should. And having a wealthy friend for emergencies, one who had reason to be grateful, would be no bad thing.'

Foster laughed, the answer being so close to the League's principals that he felt he was indeed with a friend.

#

That night at the concert, the Beau Monde was once more regarding Miss Delacroix and the Viscount Gascoigne. It seemed like poor sport, for they sat as far from each other as it was well possible to do in a room with sixty chairs facing a soprano and pianist who were the principal entertainment of the evening.

Mr Steel had taken the prized seat beside Miss Delacroix and was engaged in explaining the program to her, whilst some others looked on jealously. Mr Steel's efforts did not seem to be having the desired effect on Miss Delacroix, however, for she neither inclined towards him nor seemed to be interested in his translations, and it was not long before her aunt, Lady Pelleter, leaned over her and said to him in a carrying voice, 'Do not trouble yourself, sir. My niece is fluent in the French tongue and has no need of your - eh - efforts.'

Mr Hildegard Foster, the new entrant into the ranks of the Delacroix adoration society, shot out a sarcastic laugh.

Before the second set, Miss Delacroix rose to seek refreshments, perhaps, and no one was particularly interested anymore in her progress, but were engaged in laughing at the line of fools who followed her, no doubt to try to engage her in conversation while she just wanted to eat cake. She was wearing a dress of turquoise silk, that matched her eyes, and two ladies of a certain age discussed the fact that there had not been such a combination of wealth and true beauty for a long time in a London season. They almost missed the fleeting glance Miss Delacroix threw the viscount's way as she passed the row at the back of the room where he was seated. But when the viscount got up and followed also, the word passed around, 'An invitation! Surely there had been an invitation in her eyes.'

Scouts were sent out to see what happened at the refreshment table. But they were balked at the post - Miss Delacroix and Lord Gascoigne too, were absent. It might have been something to really chew over but for the absence at the same time of the tiny little shadow of a companion.

#

Delphine was in awe of how easily the viscount had gone through the ranks of admirers and spirited her and Miss Phoebe into a side room: done before the others had realised. Her Aunt Mags would certainly have realised, but she had remained seated, fanning herself with a program, and directing a footman to fetch her some fruit cup.

'Mr Rigby-Blythe has spoken to you?' said the viscount without preamble.

Miss Beauford felt herself to be in a fiery forge, as she stood between these two young persons; she chose for herself the farthest seat possible and tried not to hear what they said, or know what they were engaged in - thus she could hardly be interrogated later for the details.

'Yes.'

'Then there is an end to it.'

'I had to see you, to speak to you, to know-'

'And now you do.'

'All is well with you?' she asked piteously.

He laughed, but it was as far from a happy sound as could be.

'In matters to do with your fears for me, very well. I have found my own way out of that hell. I must thank you, if I had not had the humiliation of receiving my next month's fee unearned, I should very likely never have attempted it. But it has released me from many debts - including yours.'

'You were never in debt to me.'

'There we must differ.'

'Gascoigne, *please*!'

'I think that is all our business, is it not, Miss Delacroix? The music will be starting, though I believe I have not the taste for any more.' He turned to leave.

'You are so angry with me - can we not part friends?' she grasped at his coat sleeve and he looked down at her hand, removing it with his own.

'You have said we cannot be friends. I fear you are right.'

He left the room and she sank into a chair and let the hot tears flow.

Gascoigne left, said the scouts. The little lady companion came in and whispered something to Mags Pelleter, and she whispered in reply. The companion left forthwith, and it only took a half sovereign in the hand of a footman to know that the Pelleter carriage had been summoned and Miss Beauford left, holding up the other young lady who appeared to be ill.

An argument, said the World, certainly an argument of some sort had passed between the major players. It was all very well Mags Pelleter putting a brave face on it after the entertainment and telling everyone that her niece had the headache, but the World knew different. There was something still between the devilish Gascoigne and the beautiful young heiress, and they would yet find out what it meant.

#

Had anyone of the Beau Monde been present in a street just two minutes away from the interesting concert, they might have seen, by the light of the tall street lamp, Captain Fanshaw Redmond and a strange little man in a moleskin waistcoat. But even if they had, it would have been of little import to them. They could not know how closely related were the two events.

#

That night in two large and well-appointed bedrooms in two houses in London, Viscount Gascoigne and Miss Delacroix went over the events of that meeting again and again wondering if there could have been a different outcome.

'Her little hand,' he thought.

'His angry eyes,' she reprised.

'Her pleading look,' he thought.

'A break in his voice,' thought she.

But though they ran it and ran it in their head, like a play you return to see nightly, neither could make it have another outcome and both stayed awake long into the night.

#

Mrs Sybilla Lynfield had been up betimes, letting her niece stay in bed, feeling that the pleasures of the season had finally caught up with her. She wanted to go to a bazaar on Jermyn Street, where she hoped to buy a number of pairs of gloves for her niece, she having remarked that at least one pair of white kid gloves had a mark on them. She naturally met a number of acquaintances on her promenade, and the result of this was that she ordered the carriage to go to her sister's house in Albemarle Gardens, and bustled in upon her while she was still at breakfast.

'Why didn't you send me a note?' she demanded.

'What on earth are you talking about Sybilla? At least take your bonnet and pelisse off.'

Mrs Lynfield seemed to recollect herself at this point, 'Never mind that-' she said, while doing what her sister required, 'what happened last evening at the concert?'

'Mrs Burrell sang. What of it?'

'And my niece?'

'*Your* niece?'

'What happened between her and Gascoigne? The whole town is talking about it!'

'Gascoigne was not present,' said Lady Pelleter on her dignity. 'I did not see him.'

'Well, whether you saw him or not, he was there. And he had some sort of contretemps with Delphine!'

'Nonsense. We watched the first half of the concert, Delphine went for refreshments, though I believe it was more to escape her court, Miss Beauford returned to say she had a headache and would take the carriage home and send it back for me.'

'But what, my dear sister, brought on the headache?'

'I -! Oh my goodness, do not say they had a brawl in public - how bad is it?'

'Well it is merely speculation at the moment. I first heard it from Lady Jersey as a kind of warning that I did not quite understand. Then I met Sophy Ludgate and she had the impertinence to try to wheedle some story from me. I have never liked that woman. And she is setting it about that Gascoigne took Delphine into a private chamber and came out very angry. And this was borne out by Delphine leaving afterwards, *perhaps crying,* the vile woman suggested. I kept my cool and merely said that Miss Beauford had attended Delphine when she was taken unwell and that was all there was to it. I wouldn't have known that if Sally Jersey had not had the wit to warn me. Oh, Mags, this is bad. It is very bad indeed.'

'You should get home and pump little Miss Phoebe for information and do not let her escape you, Sybilla, for she desperately tries to shield that girl at all times. No. Wait till I am dressed. I shall deal with Miss Beauford, hopefully before she has had time to confer with her mistress.' She got up with decision and when her other sister arrived, passed her with only a - 'Disaster! Sybilla will tell you.'

Sybilla, on seeing the more compassionate face of her younger sister, broke into tears and went into her arms, 'Oh, Eloise. That girl! How are we to recover from this?' while Lady Carswell, all adrift, led her to a divan saying, 'There, there, my dear. Only tell me what has occurred.'

CHAPTER 10

Captain Redmond had been up betimes as well, and had gone to the arches near his lodging to hire a covered carriage of the most usual model. The proprietor said he would wash it for him before the gentleman's return, but Redmond said that it would suit him better to leave it as it was - a dirty, dusty carriage on the streets of London would attract no attention. But perhaps the groom could clean out the interior, he said, because his sister would be accompanying him to the country, and he knew what females were like.

The proprietor suspected a flight to the Border, and instantly asked the Captain to lay down another ten guineas, repayable on return, for he did not fancy having to look for his carriage in Scotland if this was indeed the case. The Captain was not best pleased, but there was no point in asking Foster for it, his pockets were completely to let. The young man had returned to his lodgings and packed a bag, which he had left at Redmond's house to be put onto the carriage later. (Had he not refused to look at his mail, which he had believed contained only bills, he might have behaved differently. For there was an envelope from each member of the League, with some banknotes in every one, understanding his desperation and offering him what relief they could. This even included fifty pounds from Gascoigne, who had melted his heart to his friend once he had descried his probable desperate state).

But Hildegard Foster did not know of his friends' continuing loyalty, and so he found himself very uncomfortably awaiting the arrival of his beloved to the park, his head a nice mixture of guilt, self-hatred and hope. It had only taken a last minute reference of the Captain's to some men not having the courage, and the sting of the suggestion of cowardice from one of the Duke's men was enough to have him fully resolved, (despite his reservations) to carry out the plan. *His* plan, apparently, though he could not remember making it. It was an audacious plan, for it involved doing the deed in the middle of the day, and his conscience was salved by his daring.

Miss Delacroix was late, arriving in a carriage with Mr Mark Steel, but Foster had somewhat expected this. He trusted that Mr Steel would not take the ladies home, for it was their want, after being driven, to walk around the park and then back to Russell Square. The ladies disembarked, but as luck would have it, Mr Steel decided to accompany them on foot, leaving his horses to be walked by his groom. It was not only Foster who was annoyed by this, apparently, for as he skulked in a side walk, he heard Miss Delacroix tell her swain coldly that she had very important matters to discuss with Miss Beauford and would he kindly leave them alone? He grinned as the young man with the flashy barouche fell away - and waited for his opportunity.

The call to action stifled his doubts and he heard from behind him Captain Redmond call out, 'Miss Delacroix! Miss Beauford!'

The ladies entered the narrow walk and walked along apace. Once the females were ahead of them, he and Redmond sprang out from their hiding places, and stuck a sponge with a foul smelling liquid over the mouths of their victims. There was no time for cries or struggle, Captain Redmond let his victim fall roughly to the ground and stepped over her in a heartless manner, whilst Hildegard held the precious prize of Miss Delacroix insensible in his arms. The Captain ran ahead, and by the time that Foster had carried his charge to the end of the walk nearest the fence gate, he had thrown open the carriage door. Emerging from the shelter of the park's shrubbery, Hildegarde was hidden between the open carriage door on one side and the broad person of the Captain on the other. They lifted her rather roughly to the seat inside. The young man jumped in after, and the Captain took the reins and drove off quickly - with no cry of 'Watch!' following him to alert the constables of the law.

Hildegard looked appalled at Miss Delacroix's pale face, checking that her heart still beat strong and that her breathing was regular. She looked so beautiful lying there and he tried to pose her limbs more comfortably, taking off her round bonnet and smoothing her hair. He took the reticule that swung from her hands and furtively looked inside. It contained, apart from smelling salts, a comb and some Holland water, a sheaf of a hundred pounds in bills and twenty gold sovereigns. It was insane for a young lady to carry as much on her person, but he supposed that the rich Miss Delacroix could do as she wished. Even had she lost it all to a cut-purse, he thought sulkily, she would simply replace it on the morrow.

His thoughts drifted to their other victim. Redmond had not been gentle with the older lady and he wondered if she had hit her head or broken a limb as she fell. He was suddenly glad he had brought his dueling pistol, for what he'd seen of Redmond was beginning to bother him. He could not allow Miss Delacroix to take any hurt at his hand, but how to stop him was something else. No, Fanshaw was a good fellow, he had just been taken away by the urgency to get to the carriage. But Hildegard still clung to the little stoppered bottle in his pocket. Enough to put a bigger man than Redmond down if it came to it. There was an inn in a hamlet beyond Southwark, with a vicar paid to perform the ceremony tomorrow. Miss Delacroix was of age, and a special license was in his pocket. Or what looked like one at least. No banns needed to be called.

It was his intention to keep Miss Delacroix sedated until the morrow; he would declare his love and his desire to be a doting husband; when she realised how compromised was her reputation, she would be glad to marry him.

Hildegard was not quite so sanguine as Redmond on this point. But glad or not, she would certainly marry him. He did not anticipate a happy honeymoon, but he believed that coming to know his genuine devotion she would melt towards him. As for his reservations about Redmond, well he'd take precious good care to spend the night outside Miss Delacroix's room and see she was not disturbed.

#

Miss Beauford awoke on her own, with a large lump on her head and various scratches from her fall. She did not know, at first, what to do. Look for her cousin, call for some help? But she was sure, and had a head to prove it, that her dear Delphine was gone, spirited away by one of the fiends who had assaulted them.

No. No calling for help. She must get back to Lady Sybilla and have Mr Lynfield decide what was for the best. She hailed a hackney cab and it took only minutes to arrive in Russell Square.

She entered the morning room, brushing away the concerns of the butler over her disheveled state and saw that all three aunts were taking tea.

'Delphine! Taken!' she said dramatically, then fell to the floor and knew no more.

#

The entrance of Miss Beauford, looking like a vagrant, her bonnet askew atop her curls; her face, gloves and dress marked with dirt and blood; a large lump forming on her temple, was enough to make the skin of all the ladies present crawl, but her dramatic announcement chilled their blood.

Lady Eloise was first to wake up. She rushed forward to Miss Beauford crying, 'Oh, Miss Phoebe, poor lady.'

While her sister called 'Fiennes!'

The butler had been hovering without, anticipating the command and now took the situation in hand by gesturing James, the young strapping footman, to come with him - directing him to place Miss Beauford onto a handsome settle, where Lady Eloise herself put a pillow behind her head.

'Fiennes,' said Mrs Lynfield, nearly distracted. 'Send for a doctor. And my husband. And inform at Bow Street-'

'Hold fast on that last, Fiennes. We must get the lady's story first. Bring the smelling salts and some water,' said Lady Mags taking charge, 'And Fiennes, send at once to Lord Gascoigne's house to see if he is at home.'

'What are you about, Mags? We cannot let the world know before we know more-'

'Smelling salts and a good slap will be all that's needed to know as much as Phoebe Beauford knows and that can be done in a flash. Gascoigne is not the world, and since the incident last night he must be our most likely suspect. If he is not at home, we have our answer. If he is, I still want to talk to him.'

#

Lord Gascoigne, when James the footman found him, was indeed at home. He had just come in, however, and had thrown a little man in a moleskin waistcoat into a chair in his library, telling him that *now* he would talk, God damn him.

First alerted to the spy that had been set upon him by the missive written with great deliberation by the landlord of the Three Swans, Gascoigne had enquired at the mail coach office, but found that the fellow was mysteriously missing from the waybill. The viscount, sending out spies of his own, had met with nothing. However, in Cribb's Parlour one evening he had seen a man in a moleskin waistcoat at another booth close by, attempting, in all probability, to hear the conversation at his table. He was tempted, very tempted, to haul the blackguard by the collar and throw him at the wall as a start to a conversation about what on earth he meant by spying on a peer of the realm. Wiser counsel prevailed, luckily for Mr Mosely, and he had instead had a whispered conversation with two likely lads, of transient appearance, giving them a shilling each and instructing them to follow the moleskin waistcoat in turns, with the promise of more *largesse* to come, if they reported to him or his butler Burton each night - once the waistcoat was hung on a chair, and its owner abed for the night.

It turned out that the moleskin waistcoat was called Mr Mosely and resided in Cheapside, and his movements of the day mirrored his own. Indeed, after the second day, it became apparent that he had hired fellows to follow a fellow who was following him. He kept the wide boys on for another week, just to get an indication of who Mr Mosely reported to, but it was not discovered. The roughs told Burton that Mr Mosely got away from them frequently, for if the viscount rode, so did the waistcoat, if the viscount took a carriage, so did the waistcoat and the roughs had no way of keeping up. This was, indeed, a head-scratcher, for how could the waistcoat come by horses or carriages at exactly the time needed? There seemed, at least, to be money behind this, and the viscount had become tired with the waistcoat and waited for him to follow down an alley, hid in the shadows then finally grabbed him by the shoulder and pulled him around the corner to Gascoigne House. 'Your lordship,' had said that individual with insouciance, 'very happy to meet you at last.' Gascoigne had growled and marched him, not very gently, to sit in his library chair.

'What a well-appointed room, my lord,' said that gentleman, at his ease, 'I always wished for a library, but the rib, you know. She doesn't 'old with books. Thinks there are too many ideas in them that make people soft in the 'ead.'

'You live in two rooms in Cheapside, Mr Moseley, and you don't have a wife.'

'Now, is that what your two nodcocks told you? Well, it isn't their fault. I played a little game with them, if you will. I'm surprised that they managed to come up with my name, if I'm honest. I 'ave lodgings in Cheapside while I'm on this job, you see, but my real ken is in Shoreditch, a tidy little property I have there, my lord, with the missus and five little tokens of our affection. Though Ernest, the eldest boy, is twelve now. Not so little anymore, my lord.' He laughed at this and the viscount was beginning to think that his first instinct, to throw the waistcoat to the wall with Mr Moseley's head still therein, was the best one.

Burton, at this point, entered, rather disappointed to see that the little man his master had brought in still had a whole skin. The butler had a constitutional dislike of sneaks.

'My lord, I would not disturb you, except that the footman from Mr Lynfield's house has called with a message from Lady Pelleter.'

'Have not you mixed up the houses, Burton?'

'No, my lord, I do not believe so.'

'Oh, bring him in.'

James, in his blue and gold livery, still looked a little uncomfortable, having already been made to feel two inches tall by a viscount's butler, a personage so superior to him in rank as to barely notice him. However he was tasked to do his duty and he did so.

'Lady Pelleter has asked that you come to Mr Lynfield's house immediately. If you please, your lordship.'

'I suppose Lady Pelleter to have issued a command rather than a request, but I do not feel inclined to go. I'm afraid I'm occupied by another matter at the moment, and do not have the leisure, tell her ladyship.'

James shifted a little on his feet, 'Yes sir, that is, your lordship. Only I think it might be what you might call urgent.'

'What Lady Pelleter considers urgent and what I do-' he looked at the young footman closely. 'If she wishes to see me about an incident last night, you can tell her from me that she can have my head to wash tomorrow. At the moment-'

'Not about last night, sir. It's about something that happened this morning.'

'Out with it, man.'

James looked askance at the little man on the chair who appeared to be listening keenly to his every word.

'Don't worry about him,' soothed the viscount, 'He's not long for this world.'

The little man chortled at this, and the viscount threw him a horrible look.

'Well, if you say so my lord. I'm not quite sure sir, but I think it's about Miss Beauford having a broken head and Miss Delacroix being missing.'

The viscount was already picking up the coat and hat he'd so recently lain across a library chair, 'Burton! Don't let this fellow go anywhere till I get back!' he ordered as he was striding from the room.

'Well, if it comes to that, my lord, I might know something that can help you regarding Miss Delacroix's whereabouts,' called the waistcoat

Gascoigne turned and looked at him disgustedly. 'I don't have time for this right now. Come with us. James - you have a carriage with you, I presume?'

'The tilbury sir!'

'A bit of squeeze, but we'll fit.'

'Well, there's the groom.'

'He can walk. Burton, have my phaeton harnessed and sent round to Russell Square!'

The butler bowed, and in a moment, they were gone.

#

Miss Beauford was brought round by smelling salts and true to her word, Lady Pelleter slapped her face to complete the process.

'Sit up woman,' urged her ladyship, frowning at the little woman with her terrible brows, whilst her two sisters clucked apologetically.

Miss Beauford did her best to oblige, only to fall back on the pillow as a wave of pain caused her to near swoon again.

Lady Pelleter shook her. 'Listen Phoebe. You must help us. Where is Delphine?'

'I do not know, my lady, I promise you. I remember we went down a narrow lane in the park-'

'Why?' said Lady Pelleter.

'Oh, I remember, someone called us. And then I was grabbed and some noxious sponge was at my mouth and I woke up with such a head! But I got a cab, for I knew she was gone and to create a great cry was useless, and I came home.'

'Very sensible, my dear,' approved Mrs Lynfield. 'Mr Lynfield will be home soon and he will know just what to do-'

'How long ago?' asked the ever-practical Lady Pelleter.

'I don't know - what is the hour at present?'

'It is not yet noon,' replied her hostess.

'Well, let me see,' she appeared to suffer from another bout of pain and Lady Eloise prevented Lady Pelleter from shaking her again, 'we arrived later to the park than usual. Mr Mark Steel drove us, as you know, and it must have been after eleven when we reached there.'

'How long after eleven?' barked Lady Pelleter in a threatening manner.

'It must have been fifteen minutes later, I believe. My dear Delphine remarked upon it, that it was close to luncheon. Mr Steel wished to show us his horses' points, so we schooled around the park for another ten, fifteen minutes when Delphine desired to be set down. The gentleman obliged, but wished to accompany us on our walk, and Delphine told him she did not wish it so, and we walked on. She was not very polite to him, I fear.'

'Never mind about polite, Phoebe. How long did you walk until you were attacked?'

'Oh, really but a moment. We alighted at the little pavilion as we always do, and then we were called into the path.'

'Planned then, they knew her movements. And a full half hour start.'

'Could it have been Mr Steel, if he was displeased with Delphine?'

'I don't - no, it could not have been he! When I woke up at last, I was a trying to decide what to do and I looked around the carriage way, hoping I would see her, but knowing I would not. I saw Mr Steel's yellow carriage in the distance, I am sure I recognised it. He was still tooling around.'

'Perhaps we should call at Bow Street, alert them at once.'

'And tell them what? That our niece has been abducted but we have no notion by who nor any description of the carriage?' said Lady Pelleter practically. And when her second sister looked doubtful she said, 'I promise you, if I thought it was to any effect, I would go there myself. But we would be raising a scandal for no result. And a scandal is just what this man wants. To pollute Delphine's name and thus persuade her to marriage.'

'It is too absurd. I cannot believe it. It is like the plot of a play at Drury Lane. How can he think it will work?'

'Richer women than Delphine have been ruined by scandal.'

'But there are twenty men who would marry her to save her name - she need not marry the brute who took her.'

'But if the brute suggested that Delphine went willingly, and that she had acted a wife for him? Where would your twenty men be then?'

'Oh, he would not-'

'He'll have her or ruin her. It is the only choice possible.'

CHAPTER 11.

Delphine was in a closed carriage, travelling at speed - that it was not her aunt's travelling carriage, or any other she had been in before, she knew. This conveyance had no velvet interior, she could just feel torn leather squabs that she was stretched out on, her knees bent at uncomfortable angle. Also, the whole had, beneath the noxious gas used to subdue her, a definite smell of turnips. She was doing her best not to stir, for the last times she had done so the foul sponge had been placed under her nose once more. She had heard someone knock on the box the last time she had been awake, and the voice was young and familiar.

'She's still out!' he said to the driver. 'She looks like one dead!'

'You've probably given her too much, you fool! Pah, shut that trap will you, I can smell the stuff from here.'

That time she had tried to rise, but strong hands had held her and the sponge was at her mouth again.

As she fell asleep, she wondered why the voices were so familiar.

Now she stayed still, though her legs were in a cramp and she longed to open her eyes. But Delphine had endured long evenings of sitting stock still on a chair while her mother read improving bible verses to her, or bade her stand and not talk as the dressmaker pinned and measured and took instructions from her mama. It was a kind of a game, her mama looking for the slightest quiver that she could jump on and reprimand her for. 'You are the most restless girl alive, Delphine.' Once she saw the dressmaker's pitying eyes and rejected them, still and cold once more. More often than not, Delphine won. She gained the ability to be perfectly still, and she used that now.

Once in the next minutes, hands caressed her hair - had the hand come near her mouth she was ready to bite. Then there were the sounds of the other occupant of the carriage moving in his seat, but gradually these died down. She remained still. There was a little fresh air coming in where one window had been lowered, and her head was nearest to there. She had the impression, by listening carefully, that her attacker (or one of them, for the rough voice of the driver was undoubtedly that of a gentleman, not a servant) had his head facing the other way. She heard him deeply breathing, almost as if…

She opened her eyes. The man on the other seat was deeply asleep. He had the sponge in his hand, and Delphine had judged from his breathing that he too was drugged. It was Mr Hildegard Foster. He looked very young and innocent sitting there, but Delphine did not hesitate, she swung her cramped legs to the floor, leaned over taking the man's hand with the drugged sponge and thrust it over his mouth, turning her head and breathing in the fresh air from the opposite window. He struggled for the veriest moment and then collapsed.

What to do now? Well, Delphine did not want to fall foul of the drug again, as her captor had done in this small space. She thrust the sponge into his coat pocket as deep as she could, with her nose high in the air. As she did so, she found the small stoppered bottle, half filled with liquid that no doubt held the rest of the horrid stuff. She took it and put it through the slit in her dress into one of the pockets tied to her waist.

The carriage was still travelling at a clip and while she would love to see her other captor, to know who she was dealing with, she had to make as little fuss as possible. Mr Foster had sounded concerned about her earlier. The driver had not. They were out of London, she feared, but she could not enjoy the pastoral setting, being more exercised in escape. If she opened the door and jumped she would be killed at this speed. As a wave of dizziness took her, she risked opening the window a little more.

She thought of poor Phoebe and started to tear up. This was useless. Phoebe was not the target, she was left in a public place. She would be found and aided. Perhaps she was even now in her cosy bed at home. Delphine knew she could not afford to think worse than that. She must restore her calm.

It was like her sense of neatness that she took stock of her appearance. Her hair was flattened, but tidy, her bonnet had been placed carefully on the opposite seat. Her dress and walking boots had taken no ill. She glanced at her assailant, who gently snored.

What did they mean by it? But marriage of course. Soiling my reputation, then one of them marrying me to save the day. It was afternoon, she had been in the carriage for longer than an hour, she guessed, and she supposed the curs had some place in the country where they could keep her company till she agreed. Which of them would it be? She supposed that as part of her court, Mr Foster, handsome and entertaining, might be believable as a runaway match. The other sounded older and any whiff of a forced marriage would of course make the fashionable world turn away. No, Mr Foster was the candidate. She briefly wondered that if he'd wooed her properly, would he have succeeded. She'd known him to be without funds, but that hardly concerned her. He'd made her laugh a little and he had seemed to be genuine in his admiration. As she had difficulty distinguishing between her suitors, and Gascoigne no longer advised her, she thought that he might just have been successful. She had very near been at the point where a dice throw could decide, so little did it matter. He had had the qualities she wanted. Light-hearted, kind (she'd regarded his treatment of Phoebe closely) and good-looking. She *could* have accepted him - a man who would do this!

The thought of Phoebe made her shudder. But she believed she would have awoken by now and be safe at home. Her family would be looking for her, no doubt, but it was hard to see how they could find her. She refused to panic. If ever her cold rage, honed over many years, was needed - it was now.

She listened to Foster's breathing, he was still unconscious. What was that heady, noxious stuff that could do this? She did not know, but she was prepared to knock out Mr Foster once more. If she soaked the sponge again, could she overcome the driver when he opened the door? She doubted it. His voice was deep, he sounded somehow, big. She must be a little more cunning so as to use, as the Duke of Wellington always said, the element of surprise. How long would they travel? The further from London, the more hopeless Delphine felt.

She saw her reticule beneath the prone form of Mr Foster, the jet beads sparkling a little. She removed it gingerly. She could, perhaps, write a note, wrap it around a sovereign, promising more if they went for help. Yet who of the three people she had thus far espied in the distance, would be able to read it? Her little silver notebook was unaccountably missing. Then she remembered leaving it on her nightstand and felt like weeping once more. She had to put back the reticule, but before she did she took three of the banknotes and four sovereigns, feeling that if the gentleman did not stop to take an accounting, they would not be missed. She put them into her pocket,

The aunts would know at last that the worst fate to befall Delphine was not the viscount Gascoigne of Raith.

'Gascoigne, find me!' thought Delphine. But how ridiculous was that?

#

Gascoigne of Raith and his weaselly little companion, entered the salon without ceremony, the viscount blinking for the moment at the number of persons present. For around the prone form of Miss Beauford there was now, in addition to the three aunts, Doctor McLeod from the city, a preeminent surgeon who spent a great deal of his time tending to the phantom maladies of bored aristocratic ladies; the master of the house, looking grave behind the back of the divan; and Lord Carswell, looking sentimental in his pity for Miss Beauford, hardly able to keep still and gazing frequently at his wife, as though for some clue what to do.

'Miss Delacroix has been abducted? What occurred?'

'Never mind that, my lord, where have *you* been this morning?' Lady Mags looked fierce.

'I have been catching a spy.' He nodded to the strange little fellow who had come in on his coattails and that individual grinned.

'What is the precise time this outrage occurred?' the little man said with a look at Lady Pelleter, whom he seemed to understand instinctively was the leader of the pack. She looked down her nose at him with her terrible eye, but Mr Mosely kept the cheeriest of demeanours.

'As near as we can tell, eleven thirty.' She said, not sure why she had deigned to speak.

'Then I can vouch for his lordship being nowhere near the scene.'

'I suppose one can buy someone to do the unpleasant work.'

'Mags!' said Mr Lynfield, 'Lady Pelleter - you really must not.'

'Very upset, Viscount,' said Carswell, glad to have a role, 'Doesn't know what she's saying.'

'If no one else will stand up to the great Viscount Gascoigne, then I will. Last evening you had an argument with my niece and today she is missing. Had she told you that your suit didn't prosper - for we *all* know she has cut you out - and you were so angry that you stooped to force her to your will?'

'My dear Marguerite!' interrupted Lady Eloise, 'You really must not accuse-'

'I don't mind being accused. It is false however. That was not the subject of our discussion, as Miss Beauford can tell you. She was present.'

'I really didn't hear. And what I heard, I did not understand-' said Miss Beauford.

'I do not think, Gascoigne, that there is anything wrong with asking, in the circumstance, what your quarrel was about,' said Mr Edgar Lynfield gravely.

Gascoigne sighed. 'I have no objection to telling you, but that is not the most pressing concern. Has Miss Beauford been able to tell us anything of use that can help me start to find Miss Delacroix?'

'Now *what*,' said the little weasel, emerging from behind the viscount's back once more, 'is that smell?'

Mrs Lynfield looked both astonished and offended, but the Scot's burr of the doctor answered, picking up an object and holding at arm's length. 'It's this!' he said, 'I sent a boy to look for it in the park, being very interested in what substance could subdue a lady so quickly. I would be glad of such when I am performing surgery.'

'I would put that sponge by you, Doctor,' said the little man, 'It is dangerous poison. I know a doctor in a bad part of town who uses just that when he has a case of amputation, and it works a treat at putting them out. *Spongia soporifica*, he calls it, because the Spanish sort that makes it for him named it that. Only it's difficult to control, see, and a lot of thems he puts *out* never comes back *in*, if you see what I mean.'

The ladies gasped, Lady Mags giving an uncharacteristic sob.

Gascoigne grabbed him by the arm. 'You know who makes this stuff, Mosely? Can you take me there?'

'I'd suggest we get right on it, guv'nor,' said the little man with energy, '-if your horses have arrived.'

Lynfield stepped forward and held out his hand. The viscount shook it. 'Find her my boy,' said the elder.

'I will sir!' promised Gascoigne 'Have Miss Beauford moved to her room. In the eyes of the world, she is, of course, with Miss Delacroix. No one should know other,' and in a trice he and his shadow had left the room.

'It might still be him,' said Lady Pelleter, with a sniff.

'Have you never seen, my dear sister-,' said Mr Lynfield scornfully, '-a man in love?'

#

'To Cheapside, my lord, and don't spare the 'orses.'

'Who precisely are you, Mr Mosely?'

'I'm the man who knows who sold those sponges to the vile creatures who've done your young lady wrong.'

'Miss Delacroix is not my young lady,' said the viscount shortly. 'You have that at least wrong.'

'You forget I've been following you for a few weeks, my lord. And I should just mention that I do have eyes in my head.'

'Damn you for a dastardly cur!'

'You wait till this day is finished, my lord viscount, and see then if you think so,' said Mr Moseley without abatement of his good humour.

The arches where Mr Moseley presently directed to stop the horses was not in a salubrious part of town. The groom sprang down from his ledge at the back and went to the horses heads, looking around him at several ruffians lounging in the street, saying to his master, 'I don't fancy staying here very long, my lord. The population doesn't look too friendly.'

The viscount thrust the whip into his hand saying loudly, 'Hit them with that if anyone gets too near!'

'I'd leave this to me, my lord Viscount, if you please.' And the little man strode ahead of him, heading for a shabby door halfway up the alley.

'This is no sawbones!' hissed Gascoigne.

'No sir, this is the mop who supplies the sawbones,' he said, wrenching open a door and displaying a darkened room, with a long, scrubbed wood table, and only two chairs beside; some shelves laden with many earthenware jars in a variety of sizes, each labelled with a tab tied by a coarse piece of string; and from the high ceiling, bunches of plants left drying. It was neat as a pin, as was the woman who was seated at a chair, engaged, domestically enough, in cutting up vegetables into a large copper. At least Gascoigne assumed them to be vegetables, but some were roots he had never seen before. She wore an old fashioned mop cap, a stuff gown and an apron. 'Come in, Señor Mose-lee,' she said in a heavy accent, 'I've been expecting you.'

'I thought I told you, Miss Carlotta, 'Not to sell those infernal sponges again?'

'You told me, Señor, that I was not to sell them to the surgeon - he was a fool, so I did not. I told him just how to use it, but he didn't listen.' She spat and made a strange sign with her fingers, indicating disgust, thought the viscount.

'But you '*ave* sold it elsewhere, haven't you my girl?

'There was a soldier I met in Spain, he'd seen me use it there to help the wounded,' she turned her dark eyes to the viscount, 'We call it *spongia soporifica*, because it induces unconsciousness. My family have guarded the recipe for many generations. It can be very useful in the right hands. But too much and-,' she snapped her fingers. She smiled, seemingly unaffected by her own words, but watching as the viscount's blood ran cold. 'The soldier came here, he forced me, he left no money. That is that.'

The viscount took some coins from his purse. 'Everything you know about that man and this is for you.'

'He has a big *barba*.'

'Beard,' said the viscount, 'yes.'

'But only here' her gesture took in the mouth and side whiskers, 'He is called Redmond.'

Gascoigne uttered an oath.

'You know him, my lord?'

'Yes, and what's worse, I think I know his companion in this.'

Carlotta held out her hand again, looking sly. 'I know where he lives.'

The viscount opened his purse, but Moseley grasped his arm. 'So do I, my lord, let us away!'

Carlotta screamed after them in her native language and Gascoigne, who had some grasp of it murmured, 'A heady grasp of curses, that witch.'

The little man was all business. 'No point in going to his lodging, because unless I'm much mistaken, he's long gone. We should look at the stables around there, see if he's hired a carriage.' It was not long before Mr Moseley, jumping onto the street and ferreting in various stables, found the individual who had rented him the carriage.

'I had my lad follow him a bit, to see if he took the Great North Road,' said this individual, to the ex-Runner, but keeping a respectful eye on the viscount. 'I had a feeling that he wanted it for an elopement to the border or some such. Wanted it with the dust on - to be in-con-spic-uous, finks I, and talked of cleaning out the inside for a lady. Anyway, the boy says he just went to Hyde Park, so he came back again.'

Gascoigne slapped his leg in frustration, 'He didn't see which road he took after that?'

'No, my lord, he came home. But a farrier friend of mine, who was called out to the country to see to a sick horse, ses to me this afternoon, "What's one of your carriages doin' down the Holburn Road, John, he ses, and a-going too fast for the wheels to be safe on."'

'Mr Sheppy, take this sovereign and take your lad and your farrier friend and have a drink on me!'

With a slap on the back, the viscount and his companion left, to point the carriage in the direction of the Holburn Road.

#

'A Runner, that's what you are, Mr Moseley!' said the viscount almost cheerily, 'though why anyone would set a Bow Street Runner on me has me stumped.'

'You are not far wrong, your lordship, me and Bow Street 'ave been acquainted, as you might say, for many years. But for two years now I have taken on what you might call private inquiries, and in terms of remuneration, it is very much more generous,' said the self-satisfied little person.

'How did you know of Redmond? Where he lived?'

'Well, now, I saw him follow a young friend of yours out of Cribb's parlour. He'd been watching your table cutty-eyed, as I was, and I got into my idea-pot that I wanted to know what was his lay.'

'Did you find out?'

'Something of it sir. He persuaded the young gentleman to go to another tavern with him and he got him to talk about his fight with you.'

'I was much annoyed. I said things-'

'Yes sir, so I gathered. It seemed to me that the young man was reluctant to speak of his argument, only saying his friends had betrayed him. Then he spoke of Miss Delacroix, sir, and talked of her beauty in a most affecting way.'

'And Redmond?'

'Well, he kept the glass filled and the anger gritty as we were wont to say, just feeding him his grievances back to him until he passed out on the table. Eventually they left, the Captain with his arm supporting the younger, and I followed them to Redmond's lodgings. To tell you the truth sir, I just put it aside as a waste of a night. If I knew what they were planning, I'd have come to you direct.'

The viscount sighed. 'One more thing, Mr Moseley, who was dispensing the generous remuneration in regards to your investigation of me?'

'Well, you might just say, in a manner of speaking, as it is the lady that we are following now.'

'Miss Delacroix ordered me investigated?' said Gascoigne, shocked.

'Now, what I said your lordship, was - in a manner of speaking,' reminded Mr Moseley.

'Mr Rigby-Blythe!' said Gascoigne, 'Of course!'

'Yes sir,' smiled the little man. 'You have, as they say, 'it the nail on the 'ead.'

'I suppose that he needed to be sure of anybody who had an association - a business association - with Miss Delacroix.'

'Not precisely sir. He was interested in how such a fine young man as you - Mr Blythe's words not mine - could have got himself such a reputation. He had noticed the closeness that Miss Delacroix felt towards you, for when she visited him weekly, she seldom spoke of aught else. She rather gave herself away, sir. And he was sure that between the two of you, you were making a mull of it.'

The viscount's eyes glinted dangerously. 'Mr Rigby-Price took much upon himself, and so do you. He was quite mistaken about Miss Delacroix, she had less interest in me than she has in the half of London who woo her. I fancy she felt some friendship, but in the end, even that-' He was aware that he was talking too much and added, 'Damn your inquisitive hide.'

'And you sir, did you not find yourself thinking too often of Miss Delacroix, but unable to tell her?'

'If you keep this up, Moseley, you'll be ejected and if you fall beneath the horses, the devil take you.'

'Yes sir,' chuckled Moseley.

They had asked at a cottage for the coach, and as it had not been busy that day, the woman inside had been able to tell them that they were only thirty minutes behind. The sporting equipage with the finest horses had made good time on the ancient carriage. The viscount's eyes glittered as they set off once more.

After a period of silence, the viscount said, 'What were you doing in Gascoigne Manor?'

'Just a full picture. I was always one of the sure and steady Runners. You need to get a full picture, that's what I say.'

'And did you?'

'Oh yes sir. A young man who has decreased his father's debts, who has done as much for his people as he could. A war hero who returned wounded to a worse situation, who tried to fix it, but was, I think, overwhelmed by the damage a life of folly (your father's if you don't mind me saying so) had wrought. There exists, though, one concern that Mr Blythe wished me to clear up. And I am not at all sure that as a barrier to any other connection, it will be hard to overcome.'

'Oh?' said the viscount, with an attempt at insouciance.

'Yes. That barrier inhabits the lodge on your estate.'

'You,' said the viscount in his previous threatening tone, 'leave the lodge at Gascoigne Manor alone.'

#

They seemed to be entering a little hamlet of some kind, having already passed The George at Southwark ten minutes since, but the horses must be fatigued, so Delphine thought a change must be affected soon.

Playing dead, an art Delphine had perfected over a number of years, for those occasions when her mother had entered her chamber, seemed to be the most sensible choice. She retrieved the sponge from Mr Foster's pocket holding one arm over her nose and put it beneath his nose again for good measure. She then put it back in his hand as he lay there. She lay back down herself, her head to the fresh air of the window, and tried for immobility.

She found that her suspicions were quite right, they were pulling into what looked like a dirty inn yard, for she braved a look while the driver was still on the box. He jumped down, however, and Delphine tried to stop her racing heart.

'Foster!' cried his somewhat familiar voice. 'For God's sake man - you are not asleep?' The door of the carriage on the opposite side from her head, was pulled open roughly. 'Pah!' said the voice as the smell of the poisonous sponge hit him, 'the bloody fool has knocked himself out.' Delphine herself was feeling a little heady and she fought the urge to sit up nearer the open window. 'Here you, see to the gentleman, he is unwell. The lady too, I'll deal with her.' What do you wait for, you clods?' he hissed. 'It isn't a fever, you'll come to no harm.'

He wrenched open the door at Delphine's head and she had to breathe deeply to avoid stiffening up. Could she just scream? But if all at this inn were in the pocket of her abductor she would lose her best hope. He put one arm beneath her head and lifted, pulling her forward somewhat. His head was bent towards her chest, seeking to hear her breathing, she thought, and then he put his other hand beneath her knees and carried her from the carriage. It seemed that some others dragged Mr Foster along. She felt the difference in sound and air as they entered the inn, which smelled of cooked mutton and cabbage, and a man said, 'A room has been prepared, follow me sir!'

All planned then, useless to appeal for help to anyone here.

There was a mounting of stairs, and a laying down on a coarse coverlet. 'Got you, my beauty. How much of the stuff did he give you? Ah, there's a blush on your cheeks, you'll come about. Not so high now, Miss Delacroix.'

So she did know him. Why could she not place him? When he began to open the tiny buttons on her high necked spencer, it took every skill she had not to shudder. There was a great noise of the door slamming open that stopped him.

'What are you doing there?' said a furious and shaky Mr Foster. 'If you do her a harm, I swear I'll.'

'No, no my boy. But you gave her too much, I'm just opening her spencer to give her some air.'

'Come away from there, let a chambermaid do it. Or I swear I'll-' there was the ominous sound of a hammer being cocked.

'Hildegard, my friend. Your head needs clearing. Let us leave this lady to the chambermaid. You are quite right. You are just a little confused-'

There was the sounds of feet shuffling and then the door of the chamber closing. Delphine rose like an automaton, and she scanned the room desperately for means of escape. There was a window and she could see it looked over a sort of low roof that was probably a store room. This was fortunate, for she believed that she could thus descend in two stages without breaking a limb.

'I'm going to take her back!' she heard Foster's voice say as she was wrestling with the casement, which would not open. The voice seemed very close, with longing look at the window she turned around, interested despite herself. There was a knot in the floor that made a guinea-sized hole in the wood, and though it was dusty, Delphine pressed her body down and eye against the knot. Her view was of a table in a room below. She could not see Mr Foster, but she had a glimpse from above of a thinning spot of hair at the crown that fanned out to what could only be whiskers and as he answered, it fell into place: it was Captain someone-or-other whose smile she had mistrusted and with whom she had not cared to dance. 'Take her back, after we've laid out all this gold? You must be all about in your head.'

'What we've done - I have done - is cowardly. I cannot.'

'But you mean to marry her!' objected the Captain.

'Not like this.'

'If not like this, then never. She has seen you. You cannot take her back without tying the knot. Look, I have the license here.'

'I'll keep you out of it, said the young man. 'She hasn't seen you. And I'll pay you back somehow.'

'Hah!' said the captain.

Delphine heard a movement on the upper corridor. She jumped up and onto the bed - no need to let the chambermaid sound the alarm as yet.

'I dunno about this,' said a rather wheezy voice, apparently to herself, 'Ladies in a swoon - knocked out *I'd* say with laudanum or the like, and a couple of rum customers with her.' The woman commenced to unbutton her spencer again, talking to herself all the time, 'I should be calling the justice, that's what, and if it isn't anything shifty-like, why has Ned got two gold sovereigns under his mattress where he finks I don't know he hides fings?'

Delphine decided, suddenly. She grabbed one of the hands that was opening her jacket and put another hand to the woman's mouth. 'You are right madam. They are scoundrels and mean no good to me,' she whispered

The woman squeaked a little. 'If I was to help you, Ned will kill me,' she said simply. She was a round dame, about twice Delphine's size, but though her eyes were scared, they were kind.

'He would not be angry if you gave him ten pounds after?'

The woman's eyes opened wide, 'No, I reckon he'd say I was clever.'

'Well, here is ten pounds.' Delphine withdrew the banknotes, '-and you can hide it beneath this mattress until I am gone. If I go now-' she indicated the window, '-can you tell them I am still asleep?'

The notes were taken and beneath the mattress in a trice, the woman aiding Delphine with the sticky casement. She hauled herself over it and said, 'If you can delay them further, I promise you I will send another ten pounds when I get to London.' She hunted in her pocket. 'Take this,' she said, giving her the stoppered bottle, 'If you break this onto a rag, be sure you don't smell it yourself, but leave it in their table and you might give me some extra time. Is there a vehicle I can take?'

'No, miss, there's only a gig and its out at the moment. Here Miss,' the dame said, running to a cupboard in the corner. 'Take my cape, you'll be less remarked than in your pretty clothes.' She threw it onto the roof Delphine was sliding down and the young lady caught it.

The last jump was only six feet and soon Delphine was away, pulling the cape over her startling blond hair.

#

Gascoigne and Mr Moseley asked at The George Inn, the busy coaching house in Southwark, whether anyone had seen the shabby carriage they were looking for. Neither were surprised that it was not there, for an abducted female could hardly fail to be noted at such a place, with all the world passing through its gates. Neither had it been seen, but Mr Moseley thought to ask the landlord if there were many inns here about where the patron might not be adverse to a little lawlessness in return for reimbursement. The Landlord feigned reluctance to 'dob in' another purveyor of comforts to the weary traveler, but a show of guineas garnered them the name of two establishments, one whose landlord was preferred as "a cove who would sell 'is grandma for a groat and a bottle of gin.' He reflected, 'Maybe just the gin."

The Fox and Goose was thus their best hope and they were pointed in the direction, being advised to come back to The George if they wanted to change horses, because the nags they had at The Fox and Goose wouldn't get them to London before a sennight.

Gascoigne turned the phaeton and went through the wide coach gates to the inn yard, just as a carter was about to enter, with a shrouded figure in a capacious woolen cape sitting beside him on the box.

'Gascoigne!' said the voice that he had been dreaming of hearing, 'You found me!'

The viscount pulled up, nearly locking wheels with the cart that had come forward, judging that the sporting vehicle would be out of the gates by now.

He thrust the reins into the hands of Moseley and jumped down, just as the small figure by the carter did the same.

'Are you real?' he asked as she ran to him, straight into his arms.

'Oh Gascoigne, you don't know how I longed for you to come.'

He hugged her closer, one hand pulling the hood tighter over her head, for there were a number of carriages in the yard. He lifted her and threw her up to the back seat of the phaeton, saying over his shoulder to his groom,

'Jack. Drive us out of here!'

'Me drive the young horses, sir?'

'Yes, dammit. At once.'

He leapt up to join Delphine and possessed himself of her shoulders, saying, 'Keep your head down my dear, we do not wish you to be seen with me.'

Her head shot up, 'With you? Why should I be sorry to be seen with you? Oh, Gascoigne, did you really come for me?'

'Can you doubt it?' he asked, laughing a little in his relief. 'I heard what you and Miss Beauford suffered and I set out after you. I wouldn't have got very far without my friend up there - a dashed spy that your Mr Rigby-Blythe set on me. But he has his uses. When your aunt Pelleter summoned me to accuse me of the abduction, he was able to vouch for my whereabouts. And then he knew the origin of that noxious concoction they used to subdue you -. Are you quite well?'

As the road was more deserted, she sat up, letting the hood fall back to reveal her hair and all of her lovely face. He withdrew a little, only holding her hand.

'I am never to hold hands with you, my aunts have said,' she said, looking down musingly. 'Do you think I will be forgiven if I let you hold them to stop me shaking?'

He gripped them a little more firmly, saying, 'It was Foster, wasn't it? Along with Redmond?'

'Yes. How did you guess? I didn't see Redmond until I was able to spot him through the hole in the floor of the chamber they had put me in. I pretended to be asleep you see. I'd recognised his voice from somewhere, then I saw him and understood. I refused him a dance once. Is that why?'

'No,' said the viscount decidedly, '-it is because he is a knave and a blackguard. And he will pay, I assure you.'

'And Mr Foster - I thought he liked me.'

'And I thought he was my friend.'

'Oh, but then I should tell you my lord. When I left, they were having an argument in the room downstairs. Mr Foster had realised what he had done, I think, and he had determined to return me to London. But I did not trust the other one, so I climbed from a window and ran away.'

'You redoubtable girl. It wouldn't surprise me if you'd broken both their heads with a chamber pot and left them bleeding!'

'Well I did use that horrid sponge on Mr Foster.'

He laughed and then, suddenly serious, 'If I'd lost you - I-!' He withdrew his hand. 'Where can I find these blackguards now?'

'In an inn a few miles beyond The George. I think it had a fox and a swan on the sign.'

'The Fox and Goose. Perhaps the goose was badly done.' He laughed, pinching her chin. 'The landlord of The George guessed well. We should turn the phaeton so that I can meet with Captain Redmond.'

The little man sitting on the box with the groom turned around. 'I think rather you should let me off here. I'll walk back to the George and hire myself a gig to go and keep those two under my eye, my lord. Miss needs to be in London as fast as you can carry her.'

'Drat it, he's right! Jack - stop the coach. Thanks for the guineas you spent at the George, Mr Moseley. If you apply to me when you return to London, I'll repay you.'

'Oh, don't worrit yourself, my lord, Miss Delacroix will stand the bill, via her attorney, I'm sure,' he said cheekily. 'Very liberal with expenses, Mr Rigby-Blythe. Pleasure to meet you 'ale and 'earty miss, as they say.' He doffed his low-crowned beaver and marched off towards the George, flagging down a brewers cart as he went.

'Do you think, my lord, that those two men will follow me?' asked Delphine, trying to keep the fear from her voice.

'I do hope so. Only let them catch us.' She laughed as he meant her to do, but she heard some real menace in his tone as he did so.

Delphine, seeing another coach approach from the opposite side of the road, pulled her hood up and let her head take up its place on Gascoigne's shoulder, so that her face could not be seen. To steady her, he had naturally to put an arm about her. Any bump on the road gave him the opportunity to hold her more tightly, and he almost wished that James find the potholes. They travelled this way until they reached London, she requesting a full account of Miss Phoebe's fate, and how he had found her location.

On the outskirts he took up his seat on the box, and Delphine sat like a maiden aunt in the back, her head bowed and her cape pulled over, so that no one would guess that the fashionable Miss Delacroix could be in such a shabby, shapeless garment.

CHAPTER 12

The Viscount Gascoigne pulled up at the stables serving Mr Lynfield's house in Russell Square, and left his carriage there. A young person, probably a kitchen maid, by the style of her shabby blue cloak, jumped down and accompanied him to the back door of the house. If the head groom thought it was odd that a viscount entered by the service entrance, and addressed his lordship's groom with the question, he was not surprised at the answer.

'Who knows what Quality gets up to,' shrugged Jack, seemingly uninterested. The head groom shrugged and said that was true enough. A weird lot and no mistake.

Fiennes took the disgusting cloak from her hands as she entered the hall.

'Is my aunt alone, Fiennes?'

'Not precisely alone Miss, but there's only family. She'll be glad to see you, Miss, if I might venture to say so.'

Gascoigne was behind her, 'Let Miss Beauford know at once, Fiennes, she will be out of her mind with worry.'

Delphine turned to him and quite naturally placed her hand on his arm. 'How right you are, my lord. Once more your kindness eclipses mine.'

He shook his head. 'Don't be a fool. It is just that I know she is not downstairs, I told your uncle she must be hidden until your return.'

Delphine ran lightly to the green salon, as Fiennes' arm indicated, and as she opened the door, Gascoigne heard the cries of, 'Delphine!' 'My dear girl!' 'Oh thank God!' and he followed her in, seeing her surrounded by family and wrapped in the arms of her Aunt Sybilla.

Mr Lynfield moved forward to him and grasped his hand. 'My boy,' he said simply, 'I have placed all my confidence in you. I hardly know how to thank you. You bring her home - safe?' There was a question in his eye.

'Quite safe sir.' He said with meaning. 'But I beg you will not thank me. Miss Delacroix rescued herself.'

'Where are the blackguards?'

'I did not meet them, but chanced upon Miss Delacroix after she had made her escape. But Mr Moseley is keeping an eye on them, I believe, providing that they had not made their escape before he got there.'

'That funny little man you brought with you earlier? Who is he? Do you repose any confidence in him?'

'I believe that the magistrates at Bow Street reposed confidence in him for many years.'

'Ah,' said Mr Lynfield, content. 'He was once a Runner! No doubt then, he has his ways.'

'Without him, I would not have known which road they had taken out of London.'

Mags Pelleter looked at Gascoigne and nodded, a large indication of her thanks. 'Who were they Delphine? We must-'

'I cannot yet say, Mr Moseley advised that I should not quite yet. One of them at least thinks himself free of suspicion, for he thinks I did not hear or see him. He may come back to London.'

'I,' said Lord Carswell, portentously, his good round face turning a purple colour. 'shall want a - a dashed word with them if they return!'

'Yes, yes, dear,' soothed Lady Eloise. 'Perhaps you should sit down.'

'I shall away, my lords, ladies, Mr Lynfield, Mrs Lynfield, Miss Delacroix. I must be at home for any news that Mr Moseley sends me,' the viscount said.

Delphine broke away from the group surrounding her. 'Gascoigne! Thank you!' She held out her hands to him again quite naturally, and he blushed. He saw the terrible eye of Lady Pelleter upon him, but grasped them for the briefest moment, then turned and left.

As he did so, Miss Beauford, with a bandage on her forehead ran in. He opened his mouth to ask after her condition, but she rushed past him, crying, 'Delphine!'

#

She was safe, he thought as he drove round to Grosvenor Square. That ought to suffice. It did suffice. Only that her head had rested so comfortably on his shoulder, his arm around her so warm, that he missed it now. She was grateful, yes, but every barrier that divided them before was still in place. He was still indebted to her, even if he knew he could discharge it when the house sale was finalised. He was still a man with no reputation for constancy with women. He was not gambling at present, but who knew when that bug would bite him again. His whole life was filled with hedonistic selfish pursuits. Think of *The Wed or Dead League,* conceived by him, and it would shock even the *ton* if it were ever discovered.

He could never go to her, never again see her, except from across a crowded room. He did not deserve her. Her gratitude was large, but even it would find its limits when she found out that it was he who had made the young Hildegard Foster believe that he could trick a lady of fortune into marriage. And then had made him mad enough to go further than that. He wanted to kill Hildegard, but beneath that was the guilt of what he, as the elder, had helped him become. Redmond was different. Redmond would be destroyed.

Her trust in him was cruelly misplaced, those lovely eyes swimming with tears of delight when she saw him; but nevertheless, he would treasure the minutes when they were in the carriage together, when he was almost sure she loved him, his whole, miserable life to come.

He would no doubt go to the devil, but not yet. Before that there was revenge.

#

Delphine, in bed reviewing her day, hardly able to believe that it was only ten hours ago that she had been driven by Mr Steel to Hyde Park. Poor Phoebe had the worst of it, she felt. Because as well as being used roughly by that cad Redmond, resulting in the large bump on her head and several scratches and bruises, she had the time all day to worry about Delphine.

As she lay there now, she thought less of her time with those monsters than about the time after - her reception when she came home. She realised now that Russell Square was more of a home to her than Delacroix House had ever been, and their greeting was overwhelming. She had been so surrounded in affection, the aunts and uncles so obviously relieved of care, that she came to understand that they cared for her. Even Aunt Mags, that strict, critical woman, was moved to tears and hugged her as if she would crush her bones, whilst Aunts Sybilla and Eloise had looked on affectionately. Phoebe's arrival, with no thought for her own injury and no blame of Delphine at all, had finally overset Delphine and she was pressed into a chair and advised to rest a while.

There was only one thing to conclude from all of this, she thought wonderingly - she was loved. How strange that today's awful occurrence should be the thing that should show her what had been in plain sight for months - for the first time in her life, she was loved. Her family were a checkered lot, it was true, and their foibles amused her greatly still, but they were hers.

When finally she had come to describe her ordeal, it was Lord Carswell, who had before this looked on a little awkwardly, once patting her shoulder as though it might break, who had been almost inconsolable in his fury. He had searched and searched for language strong enough, but his bountiful good-nature made it particularly difficult for him to express himself.

'I shall have to speak to those, gentlemen. Mind that, Eloise. You will not stop me!'

'There, there dear,' soothed her aunt, 'I would not stop you for the world.'

'No,' he said, somewhat mollified. Then changed colour once more, '- but this whole thing is - is a deuced - I mean to say it is a very *ungentlemanly*. I mean I can hardly believe it. I shall, I really shall, have to - dashed well have a word!'

'Excuse me,' said her Aunt Eloise, apologetically to the others, 'He is not usually so forceful in his language.'

Delphine laughed as she remembered it. Her Aunt Mags was particularly proud of her method of escape, but when she heard of Delphine giving a sovereign to the carter who took her up, she sniffed, 'More than his wage for this year, I daresay!' She dared not mention the payment to the landlord's wife.

There had been another revelation last night, one that she held close to her heart, it began when her Aunt Eloise had said, musingly, 'You were so brave, Delphine. How proud your father would be if he could see you now.'

Delphine had stilled. Her smile twisted when she said, 'My father - proud? No my sweet aunt, it is like you to think so, but my father despised me. I was not the son he hoped for.'

'What nonsense, dear Delphine,' her aunt laughed. 'Why would you think so? You were the light of your father's life. You followed him like a tiny dog and he would never see you banished to your room, though your Mama often requested it. He was never happier than when you crawled on his lap and pulled on his hair. Don't you remember?'

She gasped.

'Before his death we all saw a great deal more of you, when your parents were in London, or when visiting Delacroix House for the family occasions. Your father used to chase you around the garden for hours.'

'And take you on the lake in that leaky boat!' said Lady Pelleter, 'both of you would invariably return to the house wet. Emilia would be furious!'

Delphine remembered her walks around the graveled walks of Delacroix house, always accompanied by her bilious servant, Susan. Sometimes she looked into the pretty wild places off the proscribed route and seemed to remember some joyful place. Once she had asked her mother about being on a man's shoulders, wondering if it could have been an uncle. Her mother had stopped her dead, telling her she would have allowed no such thing.

'But why would you think-?' reprised her Aunt Eloise.

'Because,' said Aunt Sybilla, sounding as formidable as Aunt Mags, 'Emilia told her so.'

'I knew Emilia was heartless,' said Aunt Eloise shocked, 'but that she stooped to *falsehoods* - and to her own *daughter*.'

Aunt Mags' hands had grasped Delphine's once more, 'Your father adored you Delphine. I assure you, all your mother's sisters blame themselves for leaving you with her after he died. There didn't seem to be much to be done, when she told us she was too grieved to receive visitors, and after so many years our attempts to visit grew fewer. But if I'd known all I know now, my poor girl, I would have blasted down the door of Delacroix house until she would have had to admit me!'

So now she knew, for often she had asked herself, how a little part of her heart still lived warm inside her when all she had known was her mother's cruel distance. It was the part that was treasured by her Papa, a papa that loved her so much she'd kept him with her even when she couldn't remember him.

Her thoughts drifted to the other pleasant part of her day - Gascoigne's sudden appearance, as though in answer to her prayer. He had searched for her, had insisted it was all the work of Mr Moseley, but still, he had searched for her. And when she had disgraced herself by running into his arms, she blushed to think of it, he'd opened them to her and clasped her to his chest, as though he would never let her go. She'd felt, she knew it, some awful anxiety drain from him and she knew she was giving comfort as well as receiving it. He, too, cared. There was no denying it, there could be no denial from either of them. She had clung to him in the carriage, clung to the safety - and she was being comforted for more than just that day's horrors: but for the misery of the days they had been parted, the days when because she thought it too dangerous, they had no longer met as friends. Delphine had never had a friend such as he. One who made her laugh, at him and at herself, who moved her, by his sharp tongue, to a wit of her own, and relished it. It was impossible to offend the viscount, and thus she was free with him. He'd teased her mercilessly, showed her own faults to her, and had changed her life.

Tomorrow, when he came to see her, she would tell him again how grateful he was, how grateful all her family were, and make him her friend once more.

#

Gascoigne did not arrive the next day, and Delphine wondered what kept him. Though she had barely the heart for it, the family had decided that she would take up her usual pursuits the next day, for if any hint of her fate had come into the *ton*, she would be there to give it a lie. Sir Randolph Fraser came to call, and she agreed to be driven to the park, much to the disappointment of Mr Steel who arrived just too late. As Miss Beauford was ordered back to bed for the day, with instructions she be spoilt with all the sweetmeats, books or medicines she should desire, Mrs Lynfield kindly consented to accompany them, to Sir Randolph's chagrin.

But Miss Delacroix was seen in the park with Lord Fraser to his great pride, and if she looked in vain for a yellow-bodied phaeton, he could not tell. They went back to Russell Square rather earlier than usual, as Aunt Sybilla did not care to walk, and Delphine, feeling herself to have nodded at least to normality, spent the rest of the morning in Phoebe's room, reading to her from the stirring pages of the latest romance, and happily tending her bedside, adjuring her to drink her cordial, or wondering if she would rather have some wine and cake. All this made Miss Phoebe cry, protesting that her dear Delphine was too kind. Meanwhile Delphine had an ear for the door, for any letter or visitor that might arrive.

With no visitors before luncheon, for only Gascoigne was to be admitted, instructed she to Fiennes, she sat down to write a few lines to the viscount, urging him to tell her if Mr Moseley had been in touch. This was very far from what she really wished to know, but surely it would bring him around that afternoon.

She received a brief note from the viscount by return. Mr Mosely had not yet written, and he would inform Mr Lynfield at the first opportunity when he had heard anything more of the matter. He remained her servant, Gascoigne.

She looked at this missive, so formal in tone, and preferred when he'd simply signed "G" as he had with her flowers. That arrogant "G" was more like the real him than this. She ripped it into shreds and tried not to cry. It was exhausting suddenly feeling *everything*, she wished for a moment to switch it all off. *How* she would rail at him when next he called. She would insult him into a more normal response and make him tease her again.

But there was just the briefest of notes the next day to her uncle, and he informed her that Mr Moseley had been in touch and now Gascoigne was gone out of town. He was still on the business of the other day, he said obscurely, and he would keep Mr Lynfield informed on his progress.

'No word for me, Uncle?' Delphine asked, despite herself, but her uncle looked at her pityingly.

'No my dear, I expect he was too much occupied to write more. It is your business he is on, after all.'

Delphine went away then, peeved and upset. But it was not a moment before she was plunged into a panic. Had she mentioned the pistol to the viscount during the drive? She was almost sure she had, but what if he faced those men with no weapon of his own? Then she remembered that she had indeed told him about the weapon she had heard when pretending to sleep.

One minute she was high, the next minute in despair. Melting the Snow Queen, as she had heard herself referred to, was proving a painful experience.

#

Lord Gascoigne, meanwhile, was travelling the road to Portsmouth where he was reliably informed that Hildegard Foster was heading, to seek a suitable vessel to take him to France. Mr Moseley was on the tail of Captain Redmond, but foresaw that he would simply return home, as he did not believe himself to be sought at all – Miss Delacroix never having had the chance to see him, as he thought.

It was only the second inn along the Portsmouth road where Gascoigne espied his friend Foster, taking his ale at a table in the inn yard.

Hildegard's first intimation of his lordship's presence was his fist in his mouth, knocking him off the wooden bench that bordered the table and onto his back in the dust. He looked up, his hand to his bleeding mouth, and looked sick.

'Get up, damn you!' said Gascoigne after a minute.

Hildegard Foster did, standing on shaky legs as the landlord bustled forward, saying, 'Now, now, gentlemen-'

'Shut up! Take yourself off-' shouted Hildegard at this round little man wearing an apron, 'keep out of it.'

The viscount moved in again, and his fist this time struck Foster's jaw. The young man rocked, but did not fall, merely steadying his legs for the next attempt.

'Hildegard,' said the viscount, 'what are you at?'

'Hit me again, Titus! God knows I deserve it.'

The viscount stopped and threw himself onto the opposite bench, the fight going out of him. 'No more than me, Hildy. That devilish league, wish to God I'd never served you such a turn as to enroll you in that. It's my fault as much as yours - but how could I think you would-?'

'You could not, that was all me. I was desperate and I sounded off to a fellow-'

'Redmond, I know, don't try to protect him.'

'I'm not sure I want to now. I believe he - but that is to excuse myself. How is Miss Delacroix now? The sponge was eviler stuff than Redmond had me believe. I knocked myself out with it too.'

'Yes I know, you had some help there by Miss Delacroix, she put the sponge to your nose another twice, I believe. From what I've learnt now of the stuff you are both lucky you survived it.'

'I was sorry almost as soon as I did it, Titus, I promise you.'

'Miss Delacroix heard you argue with Captain Redmond. It is for that reason alone that you are not now dead. She was only feigning sleep part of the time.'

'I should give you this-' he threw Gascoigne the reticule which he had kept in one capacious pocket. 'I have kept an account of what I have used and I mean to pay her back. I had to hit Redmond on the back of the head with my pistol in order to stop him going upstairs to her again. I didn't trust him by then. When I found her gone, I took the carriage, but I fell asleep and crashed in a ditch before long. Probably the rest of that devilish sponge in my lungs.'

'No, I don't think so, the landlord's wife put opium in the wine to help Miss Delacroix gain time, she told my friend Mosely. Miss Delacroix had given her your bottle of evil, but she mistrusted the contents and used her own laudanum.'

'She knew me for the villain I am, I suppose. I even took the reticule, so that I could use the money to escape. Do you know that Miss Delacroix carries one hundred pounds on her person?'

There was a silence, which stretched a long time, while Foster righted the bench and sat on it, hanging his head as though he were regarding the chickens that scratched in the yard. Gascoigne knew better.

'So what was your plan?'

'Oh, I hardly know. To get out of England and find Wellington's army and join the ranks, I suppose. I don't know why they'd take me. I'm too cowardly to accept my fate in London, or to wait for the Runners to find me.'

'In a way, one already has. But there is no one else looking for you, Hildegard, Miss Delacroix knows that you wanted to let her go. She has not quite forgiven you, but she does not wish you to be pursued. I suppose you could come back to London, if you chose.'

'I could not see her. I could not.'

'You cared for her and yet you did this thing.' He was silent. 'But I believe the prime mover was Redmond.'

'No, apparently I had outlined a plan before I passed out that night.'

'That cannot be true. My friend Moseley was there and heard all you said. You made no such plan.'

'Then it was all Redmond-. But no, *I* still did it.' He put his head in his hands.

'Yes.'

'I'm going to France. I'll stowaway if I have to. Joining up is the only answer.'

'Even if you can't buy your commission, there are many ways to advancement in time of war. I'll write my friends to have an eye on you.' He held out his hand. 'Good luck Hildegard. I'm sorry for my part in your downfall. I hope you rise again. I believe you can.'

He took out three guineas from his own purse and left them on the table. 'A loan,' he said briefly, 'I expect it back before three years are up.'

Hildegard gave a harsh laugh, and Gascoigne left him.

#

The moleskin waistcoat was patted in a gesture of self-satisfaction. Captain Redmond was now abed, sleeping the sleep of the unwary, whilst Mr Moseley stood beneath his casement window. He'd considered his options and his decision was to return to Cheapside and sleep the sleep of the just. There had been many possibilities, including surprising the gallant Captain in bed - armed with his barking-irons, or bringing a crew of Runners to take him in - but he had rejected them. The first would deny Gascoigne the outlet for his rage, and the second might cause the young lady's name (discreet as the magistrates could be) unwanted speculation. Of course if she was to be a viscountess pretty soon, there would be no scandal, but he had an idea that those two souls, who obviously belonged together, might still make a mess of it.

A word to Mr Rigby-Blythe, who seemed like a sensible person, might be in order.

CHAPTER 13.

Delphine had a letter from Gascoigne the next morning, which inflamed her spirit. She wanted no more letters, but only to see him. *Why* did he not come? She ripped it open.

My dear Miss Delacroix,

I have to tell you that one of the men concerned in your business, the younger of the two, has left for France. He begs that you will forgive him and has returned your reticule to me, which I will send with this letter. I know that you did not wish him to suffer the full judgment of the law. I believe him truly penitent and he goes to fight in the army of Wellington, without a commission, hoping to work his way to respectability once more.

On this matter, there is also this to say. It was I who led such a young and pleasant youth onto the cynical path that has ended in this base behaviour. He is penitent, but I am more so. Though I could not guess where it would end, mine is the largest part of his culpability.

The other man is under our hand, do not fear.

I trust that you and Miss Beauford are fully recovered.

I remain your servant,
Gascoigne

He had led Foster down a path to abduction and forced marriage? It was not possible.

She remembered the day was Thursday, and knowing that she could not expect the visit she hoped for, she decided that she and Phoebe, who had left off her bandage and declared herself fully recovered, take a cab to her regular appointment to her lawyer's office.

#

Mr Rigby-Blythe had received a late night visit from Mr Moseley and was thus overjoyed at Miss Delacroix's unlooked for arrival.

He rose from his chair with more alacrity than she'd thought possible, and he hurried to greet her as she made the outer office.

'Miss Delacroix! My dear girl - I'm so glad to see you unhurt. And Miss Beauford, you too. My clerk will fetch some refreshment. Could you fancy some hot rolls, or just some tea perhaps?

The young lady followed him into his inner sanctum whilst Miss Phoebe sat at her usual place, with the chatty clerk seeing to her comfort.

'My dear! I'm glad I did not know of your abduction until you were quite safe. I'm not sure my old heart could have taken it.'

She leaned up to kiss him, an attention that made him smile. 'Well, well, my dear,' he said patting her arm, 'you are safe now.'

They took their accustomed seats and Delphine realised how much she had loved visiting this slightly dusty old room, with the pile of documents in precarious heaps, the friendly fire crackling in the grate with the kettle set there for making tea, the filthy window behind Mr Rigby-Blythe's chair keeping all their secrets within. She had always, even before she'd understood her aunts' genuine affection, felt cared for here.

'I suppose I should begin with Mr Moseley. It seems we were lucky that I had employed him, but you'll want an explanation of why I did not ask you.' He gave her the wise regard under his eyebrows again, almost apologetically. 'The trouble was, I really liked the viscount. And I had to understand how a young man like that had come to such a pass as to accept your curious bargain. And if *I* liked him, and I was not-'

'A susceptible young woman - I take your meaning. But it was, as I told you, a business arrangement.'

'Indeed, but even if you ignore his good looks, his rank and his charm, you talked a little too often about his amusing remarks-'

'You thought me in danger?' she said, a little too brightly. 'You were quite right.'

The old man's eyes watered in concern and sympathy. 'So I just wished, since you yourself said you needed all the facts on your suitors-'

'To make sure I had the facts on *him.'* She nodded, looking down. When she looked up again her expression was open and raw. 'Will you accept instruction from me, Mr Rigby-Blythe?' He nodded. 'Will you never tell me what you found out? I do not, not ever, want to know all the facts about Lord Gascoigne.' Mr Blythe sat back in his seat, amazed. She smiled up at him, eyes twinkling, if a little sadly. 'I fear it would make no difference at all.'

'I quite understand, my dear.' And he smiled. But still in his head he worried, what about the lodge at Gascoigne Manor?

#

The inhabitant of the lodge at Gascoigne Manor was at that time travelling by stage to London, bowed down by the rumours she had heard about Titus and his interest in Miss Delacroix, and also the talk of the snoop who had been asking so many questions about her. This time Gascoigne would not fob her off, she would make him tell everything. She hugged the child with autumn coloured hair to her breast. The little boy stirred and snuggled. She worried for his future. Gascoigne had made her promises, but-.

#

Captain Fanshaw Redmond, very much at his ease, though several guineas the poorer on account of the abduction scheme, wondered if he might go to the park for a short walk and a nod to the ladies. He would go nowhere near Miss Delacroix, however. He knew that he had no hope there, and that she would now be closely guarded - but there were always other young ladies of the Beau Monde who might find a gallant captain of the Hussars a heroic figure. Marriage had never been an object of the captain's but having left the service he was finding it increasingly hard to fund his predilections. It was certainly true that being a soldier had expenses - the uniform of an officer with its gold braid and sharply tailored fit, plus his sword and other kit were more expensive than his coats from Shultz the tailor. But one needed rather more in the way of wardrobe in civilian life: the riding coats and cripplingly dear riding boots, his hunting accoutrements, ballroom suit with its knee breeches and silk stockings, his normal day wear (several sets) and the fashionable *pantalons* necessary for dinner with friends and so on. He had forgotten how expensive life outside the army could be, so a woman with a comfortable income he must find. He was aware, that as a man of forty his good appearance was fading. He may have to look to an heiress whose father was a cit, or some northerner in trade. His uncle was a baronet without issue, so the captain offered a prospective title for sale.

He was thinking this as he walked, for though he rued the loss of Delphine Delacroix, and had been in a rage at the collapse of his carefully planned scheme due to Foster's cowardice, he was a soldier who put the last campaign behind him and went onto the next. Doubts at the last moment! If he ever saw him again, he would pay Hildegard Foster back for the lump on the head. He'd woken up some minutes later, to a missing carriage and two missing companions. It did not take him long to discover that Foster had gone off on his own, the girl must have escaped. The idiot had only one job to do, thought Redmond bitterly, and he bungled it. So the captain had hired a gig with the last of his money - but recouped some after he found the London hire carriage in a ditch two miles from the inn. It was not damaged. And he was able to change horses at the George, and drive to London without more expense.

He now traversed an alley on the way to the park, not salubrious, (for his lodgings were on the very edge of the polite world and bordered more mean streets), but certainly a shortcut to the broad thoroughfare beyond.

A familiar voice said, 'Good morning Captain, well met sir!' He saw that a little fellow blocked his way at the end of the alley. He vaguely recognised him, by the moleskin waistcoat, as a chatter-box who had insinuated himself into conversation with him in some low tavern, and also once on the street. The oddness of meeting him for the third time, and being hailed as a friend, suddenly struck the captain. He stopped to brace himself for trouble, but he was too late, for while he was distracted by one, another came up behind and he heard the rush of air as the cudgel hit him on the head.

He awoke in the library of a great house. Judging by the handsome figure on the edge of a handsome walnut desk, it was Gascoigne House. The viscount was regarding him coldly, one of his legs was swinging carelessly, the captive noted, but the other planted on the ground ready to spring. Redmond thought idly how much he had wished to receive an invitation here, to be in the inner circle of the fashionable viscount. But now, he did not think he would be asked to dine.

'He's awake!' said a familiar voice behind him, as though delighted that he had taken no hurt.

'So I see,' said Lord Gascoigne. 'You can go now, Moseley.'

'I don't think so, my lord. That might not be so safe for anyone.'

The Captain heard a bustle in the hallway and a voice he knew, vaguely, saying, 'Get out of the way man, do!'

The viscount eyed the man behind the chair narrowly. 'What did you do, damn you?'

'Saved your immortal soul, my lord,' said the ever cheery voice behind the chair.

Redmond was predisposed to think that anyone entering the library, which the crowd in the hall seemed to want to do, was good for him. Anything better than being left with the steel-eyed Gascoigne. But when the door opened, he closed his eyes briefly in disbelief. For in walked a number of men, the first two Mr Lynfield and Lord Carswell, uncles of the Delacroix girl, with three other darkly dressed individuals, who bore all the appearance of Bow Street Runners. The game, then, was up.

'Guv'nor! What are you doin' 'ere?' asked one of the younger officers.

'Lord, I ain't yer guv'nor no more, young Malahyde. But you lot might wait outside for my call.' he added as the men automatically did as they were told. He finally came forward into Captain Redmond's view. 'And if you was to hear any other cry but mine, I shouldn't heed it,' he said, belaying their exit. 'This 'ere gent abducted a young lady. And these fine gentlemen, whose names I pray you will forget, are the relations of same.'

Young Malahyde, his cheery manner a match for his old boss, answered for them all. 'Deaf and blind, we are guv'nor.'

There was a brief silence as the door closed. It was a very different Mr Lynfield from his drawling, usually suave, demeanour that Captain Redmond had the joy of seeing. This man was cold and full of rage, and strode forward, 'You!' he said vengefully.

The viscount, held him back. 'I, who caught him, claim the first privilege.'

'Sirs!' attempted the Captain, spluttering.

'Shut your potato trap, pie-face,' instructed the one called the guv'nor.

From behind the viscount, a shaken, blustering voice said, 'I - I want a word with you, you dashed bounder!' The other gentlemen in the room exchanged a look of amusement - but in another second, Captain Redmond found a devil beside him, with bulging eye and purple face, whose circling arm caught him on his jaw with enough force to push it from his socket - and for him, and the heavy chair beneath him, to be upended on the floor. Redmond held his jaw and screamed in pain.

'Good God! Pinky!' said Mr Lynfield.

'Told you I wanted a dashed word!' said Lord Carswell, standing over the chair with satisfaction.

In a second, the tension in the room broke like a dam, Mr Moseley, the viscount and Mr Lynfield burst into guffaws of laughter, having to hold each other up in their hilarity.

#

That evening, Uncle Edgar took Delphine aside. 'My dear, the other culprit has been dealt with. He has been taken into custody and the magistrates have assured me that your name will appear nowhere on the charge. If he utters any word of you, it has been made plain to him that it will go the worse for him. He was apprehended by Lord Gascoigne and the detective Mr Moseley. A most interesting little man.'

It was important, she knew, to be unaffected, for if the world guessed that she was the victim, then there would indeed be gossip. So that evening Aunt Eloise called and took her to Almacks. She danced with all her beaux and enjoyed Miss Beauford's energetic attempts at dancing, and searched the room all night for one who did not come.

She had become the cold, detached Miss Delacroix once more, though she herself did not notice it.

The next morning, and still no word from Gascoigne. Still he did not come. What did he mean by it? That she could not at least express her gratitude was insupportable. Three days and all she had were two cold notes. Had she dreamed his arms about her, his kind compassion? That was it. He was compassionate. It was no more than that. No doubt the speaking looks she gave him were embarrassing for him. She had given herself away totally, he knew how she felt and unable to return it, was keeping out of her way. Their business was finished. He'd returned some of the money so as to get out of the awkward situation of attachment to a green girl who could only buy his love.

She would not let him see her hurt. No one could know it. She was pacing the salon as she thought these things, and noticed Phoebe regard her worriedly. 'Let us go out for a while, my dear. I think that I need another shawl now that the evenings are so cool. And you too, Phoebe. We have both worn one shawl throughout the season. Do you think Waithman & Sons or Clark & Debenhams would have the better choice?'

Since Miss Phoebe had little to say to this, not being yet an expert on shopping in the bazaars of London, Delphine asked her aunt before they left.

An hour later, invigorated by the walk and the shopping trip, Miss Delacroix espied a familiar yellow-bodied phaeton. She had almost raised her arm to hail it, when she saw on the box beside Viscount Gascoigne, the most beautiful woman she had ever seen. The viscount saw her and gave a stiff bow of the head, not lingering on her startled face.

Mr Moseley could have told her, had he been present, that in this dark-haired, exotic-eyed beauty she was looking at the inescapable barrier to her joy, the inhabitant of the lodge at Gascoigne Manor.

Somehow, though she had not that piece of the puzzle, Delphine knew all her hopes were dashed.

CHAPTER 14

Delphine's mood ran from white hot to ice cold. She was as incapable of confiding in Phoebe as to her aunt, both of whom had asked what was wrong. She'd answered with a terribly bright, 'why nothing at all, my dears' that had terrified them more. As she dressed for the evening's entertainment, a great ball at Lord Grandiston's, her laughter was tinkling and brittle. Her insistence on the details of her ensemble, meticulous.

The coils from which her silver ringlets fell were rather higher this evening and the placement of white rosebuds around it very precise. She wore a simple white satin dress with a two foot train and a stiff lace collar standing around the back and shoulders in a regal touch. A shawl of silver net embellished with white rosebuds and a pair of silver slippers finished it off. The snow queen had returned, thought Miss Phoebe in alarm, and she was a dangerous goddess.

Miss Phoebe wore a simple, but rich, brown silk and a paisley patterned shawl, such as she had never possessed, while Aunt Sybilla a regal purple, with long violet gloves and a similarly coloured shawl.

Delphine's carriage chatter was light, with the strange trilling laugh she had adopted only in the last two days. Her aunt guessed what was wrong, and she and her sisters, who had discussed the whole situation at length over tea, were at a loss how to help.

The Ball was a grand affair. The Earl of Grandiston and his beautiful Countess, once the heiress Oriana Petersham, welcomed them warmly, and Mrs Lynfield had never thought to see such beauty as the countess and her niece standing together, one with hair of spun gold and a dress flecked with gold embroidery, the other a silver princess. The two young ladies promised to exchange words later, and then the party moved into the ballroom.

It did not take long to spot him. The Viscount Gascoigne, his autumnal locks tumbling artfully over one side of his brow, his muscular body encased in knee breeches, white silk stockings and a black coat that had been made by a master to reveal his frame, stood laughing with a number of friends at the other side of the ballroom. Miss Delacroix turned to Miss Phoebe and gave a trilling laugh for nothing at all.

It seemed that the viscount heard, for he came across towards them negligently, stopping to say a little something to friends along the way.

By this time, Delphine had around her some gentlemen asking her to dance. Mr Steel was on one side, Sir Roger Fentimen on the other. While her cousin, Foggy Carswell, was edging in, saying in a lowered tone, 'Dashed sorry I missed the excitement, Delphine. I was out of town. Dance with me and tell me all - out of the way of these rattles.'

Miss Delacroix paused, waiting until the viscount was almost upon them before saying, 'Come on, Foggy, we'll miss the waltz.'

Carswell spun her out, and for one second she could see Gascoigne make one of the dispirited bunch of suitors, before he asked Phoebe for her hand. Miss Beauford's overly energetic enjoyment of the waltz, the first she had danced, gave Delphine a nip of sour pleasure. Foggy was asking questions about the abduction and Delphine related the whole as an amusing tale, and had Foggy Carswell laughing at the history of the sponge in the carriage. She refused to name the culprits though, so Foggy finished the dance with a darkling look, swearing he'd get her to tell him sometime. Because he wanted, he said, a *dashed* word with those blighters.

This little theatre of heady enjoyment had mostly been wasted, for Lord Gascoigne, pleading a need for refreshment, had led Phoebe to the supper room. Mr Steel had her hand next, but only for a country dance where they were almost always parted by the steps and he could not ask what he had determined to. That she looked more beautiful than ever this evening, he did manage to say, and Delphine replied to him in her old, shockingly honest manner. 'Yes, that was my intention.' But Mr Steel acquitted her of vanity. She had the air of someone stating the truth. They met Phoebe and his lordship - her companion chattering away with him warmly - coming from the supper room as they were entering and they stopped and bowed. 'May I have this dance, Miss Delacroix?' the viscount asked politely.

'I am on my way for refreshment as you see, my lord,' Delphine said icily.

He dropped Miss Phoebe's hand abruptly and said, taking hers and pulling at it a little towards the floor, 'You can wait. Mr Steel can escort Miss Phoebe back to your party.' He added over his shoulder.

It was another waltz, and Delphine damned the cursed orchestra under her breath. As Gascoigne swept her onto the floor, she adopted the most frigid of tones to say. 'Your companion today was very beautiful. A Spanish lady, perhaps?'

'She was not what you think, Delphine.'

'How do you know *what* I think?' she asked crossly.

'It was written all over your face when you saw the carriage today,' he answered a trifle wearily, 'But I wanted to ask you how you are after your ordeal and to tell you that you will not see the culprits again.'

'So you will not tell me more of your lovely companion?'

'No.'

'No? Oh, I beg your pardon. I believe there are certain types of females gentlemen do not discuss with ladies.'

'Behave yourself.'

'I beg your pardon?'

'You shouldn't speak so and you know it.'

The trilling laugh again. Delphine looked off to the side, where she saw her Aunt Sybilla and Miss Beauford had been joined by her Uncles Edward and Carswell, Foggy, Aunt Eloise, and finally Lady Pelleter, all regarding her and Gascoigne as if they were they were the two headed dog in a penny booth at the fair.

'They are all watching us.' She nodded her head in the direction of her family.

'Probably asking themselves what new scrape the dastardly fortune hunter Gascoigne will inveigle you in.'

'No! They are all grateful to you, as am I. And you were never a fortune hunter.'

'You are wrong. From the first I told you I was.'

'Only because it was beneath your dignity to hide from me that it was low tide with you.'

'Yes, but I expected that my partial honesty, good looks and affable charm would prevail and I'd steal the fortune after all. I have always been well set up in self-regard.' She heard the bitterness in his voice.

'Your eyes always on the riches, eh, my lord? I do not believe you.'

'Oh, my eyes moved elsewhere, I assure you. My lord Alvanley remarked to the Prince that even had you been a pauper you would have been the belle of this season. You are remarkably beautiful.'

'And yet, my lord, you are no longer interested. I have money and beauty but you found me myself wanting. I think I understand.'

'Please will you stop it, Delphine? You know it could never work - you've said it enough times. I do not have the qualities you want in a husband.'

'And now there is *another* reason you do not call on me or write any but the coldest letters. Dark hair and exotic eyes.'

'You were grateful and we found each other again,' he said in a removed voice, 'but that is all. I cannot shackle you to a broken horse. Believe me it is for the best.'

The dance finished and the two broke apart, Miss Delacroix with a heaving chest and too-bright eyes and the viscount looking as dark and dangerous as the world had ever seen him. She did not wait for him to take her hand and lead her to her aunt, but left the floor. Gascoigne turned abruptly in the other direction, with a face as black as thunder as the Beau Monde gasped. The sporting event was on again, and the odds on Gascoigne were shortened or lengthened, depending on how the audiences viewed this latest drama. 'They cannot now claim to be nothing to each other,' said one Lady Nip-cheese to some Mrs Poke-nose, who answered, 'No indeed!'

'Get him!' said Mr Lynfield, to Foggy Carswell. 'Bring him to the library, if you have to knock him out to do it.'

Foggy took this ridiculous rider as the exaggeration it was, and went to seek the viscount.

#

Mr Rigby-Blythe and a little companion wearing a moleskin waistcoat were in a warm and cosy tavern, toasting their feet by the fire contentedly and raising a glass to the success of their collaboration.

'I suppose,' said the sagacious attorney, 'that we should not, as it were, count our chickens,'

'Well, as to that, my friend, (and I 'ave never afore thought to call no jaw-cove my friend) I have rarely seen a runner I'd rather bet on than Mr Lynfield, he's what you call a stand-up-Jack. I'm betting he can pull it off if anyone can.'

'Hard-headed, his lordship.'

'As is the young miss. 'Ard-'eaded and warm 'earted.'

'Here's to them!' said Mr Rigby-Blythe, his watery old eyes overflowing, 'May my sad little angel - for such she was for too many years, Mr Moseley - may that poor little girl know love at last!'

#

It took a bit of time for Foggy Carswell to do the necessary. Gascoigne, set on leaving forthwith, was searching for his hosts to bid them goodbye, whilst various friends accosted him en route, with a few words about a race meet or a horse, or a sporting event. Foggy followed him with dog-like persistence saying, 'But I assure you old man, I *must* grab a word right now. Matter of the greatest importance.'

'To me?'

'I - well - not really sure,' said Foggy, pushed to the wall, '-but I expect so.'

'Foggy what *are* you talking about? Do you want to tap my shoulder or something?' he asked, using the cant expression for borrowing money.

'No, no,' said Foggy, embarrassed, 'just need a word, that's all.'

The viscount stopped. 'Not a *dashed* word by any chance?'

Foggy frowned. 'Don't think so - what?

'I'm relieved,' Gascoigne said, continuing through the throng, 'Fisticuffs are beyond me tonight, I just want to get away from this damned ball.'

'Fisticuffs? Gascoigne, really no. In point of fact, I wouldn't dare and why you would think-?'

'Inherited traits are not universal, then. Stop frowning Foggy, I'm joshing you.'

'Yes, but Gascoigne I assure you, most faithfully, that we really *must* have a word in the library.'

The viscount had just spotted his quarry, Lord Grandiston, then looked down at Foggy. 'Can't it wait till tomorrow, Foggy?'

'Well, I suppose-' said the good mannered Foggy, and then, remembering his remit, 'that is, dash it, no!'

Gascoigne stopped and shrugged. 'This had better be good. There is no one I want to speak to at the moment, so keep it brief.'

He entered the library to find it full of aunts.

'What the devil-?' Gascoigne turned on his heel and headed for the door. Foggy Carswell blocked his exit, however, dodging from the waist like a pugilist avoiding blows. 'Foggy! For G-' He breathed deeply, and turned back to the assembled company, not before lightly clipping Foggy's ear, with the flat of his hand, on the way.

'Ow!' said The Honourable Mr Carswell, but grinning.

'Ladies, how can I serve you?' said Viscount Gascoigne of Raith, at his most majestic.

'Sit down Gascoigne!' said Lady Pelleter, who though no higher than his chest, was still a formidable opponent.

The viscount sat. The library was an apartment much like his own, with scores of leather bound volumes on the shelves, heavy furniture of a previous age, leather covered furniture and a couple of large desks on opposite walls. Grandiston had a secretary, he remembered, hired to research his speeches in the Lords. It was rather larger than at Gascoigne House, of course, and well able to accommodate the three dames facing him as well as the timid Miss Beauford, seated in a corner. Perhaps Miss Delacroix was absent from this meeting because it was the family's final *congé* to him, unnecessary and futile.

'I assure you ladies, you have no need to tell me what you brought me here to say - I know it all and I ass-'

'Be quiet, Gascoigne,' said Lady Pelleter, as to a naughty infant.

There was a tense silence, broken only by the occasional embarrassed moan from Foggy's corner, till his Aunt Mags also frowned him down. The library door opened and another clutch of Delacroix relatives entered, along with a confused Miss Delacroix.

'But Uncle, I *do* have the headache, and I wish to go home.'

'You are giving *me* a headache,' her good Uncle Edgar drawled, 'please do as you are bid, Delphine.'

This, from a previously indulgent voice, kept Delphine silent with shock. She looked back at her Uncle Carswell, who patted her arm in his bluff manner and said, 'There, there my dear. In you go. Take it on the chin, what?' She frowned at this, then looked where she was going and saw the viscount, seated on an impossibly large chair, with her aunts ranged around, and came to a full stop.

'My Lord!'

'Miss Delacroix!' he said springing to his feet.

'What is this?' said Delphine, addressing the room, but unable to take her eyes from the viscount's.

He broke the link, saying, 'I imagine we are here to listen, as a finality, to all the reasons that make me a bad bet for a husband. If you can end it by saying that you already know, Miss Delacroix, we might now be free to go our separate ways.'

Mr Lynfield now came forward, leaning on a desk facing him in a way that mirrored Gascoigne's own position when he had Redmond at his mercy, 'What you *imagine*, Gascoigne, is not of any interest to me. Sit down.'

Again, Gascoigne obeyed, though why he could not say. He attempted to, though. 'I suppose if I try to leave, his lordship will have a *dashed* word with me.'

Lynfield smiled briefly, but turned to Delphine, 'You too, miss.' Delphine obeyed. Her uncle regarded her gravely.

'I have tried, Delphine, to leave you to your own affairs since you entered my home. I believed, perhaps wrongly, that you had had enough interference in your young life and I merely wished for you to have a happy time in London. This was also true of your aunts.' Those ladies nodded grimly.

'Thank you, uncle. But what has this to do-'

'When you became involved with Gascoigne, I had the same concerns as your aunts, I suppose.' Gascoigne's face was frozen. 'But regarding the pair of you initially, then it seemed to me that you had entered into some other relation with his lordship, one hardly based on romance. I also had reservations about jumping to conclusions about Gascoigne. He had never before pursued an heiress you see, however much the world knew him to be in debt.' Delphine opened her mouth. 'You do not have to tell me my dear, I have had a chat with your attorney this morning, so I understand the substance of your arrangement.'

'I do not!' said Lady Pelleter. 'What arrangement?'

'It hardly matters now,' said Mr Lynfield with finality. 'What matters is that however difficult for me to admit, in matters of the heart, my wife is *always* right.' Lady Sybilla audibly purred. He looked at Delphine squarely. 'You became infatuated with the viscount.' She blushed and gasped, hardly daring to look at Gascoigne.

'You are wrong sir, Miss Delacroix remained the same. She terminated our arrangement and sent me off.'

'Have you not heard, my lord,' said Lady Pelleter largely, 'that the women of our family are *never* wrong?'

'I think he said that that was *me!*' said Mrs Lynfield, sotto voce.

'I should rather have said, you became mutually infatuated,' apologised Mr Lynfield.

'Ha!' said Delphine, caustically, 'I believe his lordship has more than *one* infatuation.'

'Before we go any further, Delphine, I should say two things. One, that I persuaded Miss Beauford to tell me what ailed you today.' Delphine exchanged a look with her companion who mouthed *so sorry!* 'And second: that before I came here tonight I went to Gascoigne House to resolve Mr Rigby-Blythe's last mystery. I saw the occupant of the Lodge on the Gascoigne estate.'

'Occupant of the Lodge? Oh that is famous!' cried Delphine rising. 'I suppose she has exotic dark eyes?'

The viscount did the same, saying, 'It is no one's business-'

'Quite.' Said Mr Lynfield, 'but I beg you will forgive me, my boy. Mrs Taylor required me to share her story with Miss Delacroix. Indeed, she feared that Gascoigne would keep her secret, even to his own ruination.' He smiled, 'Lord Gascoigne's father was everything Gascoigne is rumoured to be and more. He had a daughter, not with his viscountess, and left her and her mother destitute. She was very beautiful, as you saw, and she married a young lieutenant in the guards. When he was killed, she found herself alone again, this time with a child to feed. It was at precisely this moment that Gascoigne, going through his father's papers, made enquiries for her and brought her to live at the Lodge. It has caused some talk in the village and on the estate, and she has offered to leave many times, but Gascoigne won't hear of it.'

Delphine looked at the viscount, but it seemed he could not meet her eye.

Lady Pelleter pulled Gascoigne's coat once more to make him sit. Her niece was looking at her, now sitting on the edge of her seat.

'I don't understand. Did you bring me here to tell me again why I cannot marry him?'

Lady Carswell joined her husband to say, 'No, my dear. We are here to say, that sometimes-'

'Only *sometimes*, mind' added Aunt Mags.

'-your aunts can be *very* wrong.'

Delphine jumped up and embraced her, and then her uncle Carswell who blushed and looked pleased.

'Perhaps,' said Foggy, somewhat confused, '*he* don't want to marry her.'

'Pah! By all accounts he wanted to kill the man who took her,' said Lady Pelleter.

'And,' said Aunt Sybilla, reasonably, 'You can't go arguing with young ladies on the ballroom floor, losing all the dignity of your ancient name and great rank, if you are not in love.'

'And cuddling me all the way to London, don't forget that!' added Delphine.

'Goodness!' her Aunt Eloise protested a little, but her husband patted her hand.

'Oh,' said Foggy, 'So that's how it is.'

Delphine was smiling at the viscount, standing a few paces away from his chair, and that smile lit up the room.

'I think he minds about Delphine's inheritance, you know,' said Miss Phoebe from the corner of the room where everyone had forgotten her.

'Precisely! And if *we* don't mind any more, knowing what we know - why should *he*?'

Gascoigne was no longer listening, instead pressing himself into the chair and looking at Delphine, in her white dress and sparking shawl, as though she was a primed cannon.

'So now that it is all resolved, when can we marry, my lord?' She took a step towards him and Mags Pelleter gestured the others out, they rose as one, making their way to the door.

'Delphine - Miss Delacroix, I am still the same fortune hunter, the same man-' he protested.

She took the next step, her eyes never leaving his. 'Then we have still an account outstanding, my lord. I must marry,' she said, standing over him now - so you must advise me - shall it be Mr Steel, with his upright mind and no sense of humour?' She sat on his knee and he gasped. 'Sir Roger Fentimen, who wishes to teach me to fish at his castle in Northumberland?'

He held her tightly, 'Careful, my dear, we cannot-'

'Or the Reverend Mr Wright, who wishes to read improving literature to-'

'Oh, my God, Delphine!' he said kissing her neck in a way she much approved of, 'I give in. If I must, I must!'

In only three minutes, they were interrupted by a tentative knock and Miss Phoebe's head appeared around the door. 'Oh, good,' she said observing them, 'it's settled. Only your Uncle told me to come and get you. The orchestra stops after the next dance you see.'

'For what purpose?' asked Delphine, dreamily.

'Why to announce your engagement, of course.' The little lady left and closed the door quietly.

They got up, Delphine dragging the viscount by the hand.

'The announcement is to quash the scandal of our behaviour on the dance floor, I expect,' said the viscount, 'Probably everyone now thinks that your family have forced me to do the decent thing.'

'Probably!' Delphine turned to find herself once more in his arms. 'They will think I bought myself a Viscount.'

'And so you did my dear, heart and soul.' He engulfed her in an embrace that she never wanted to end, then he led her, protesting, to join the family for the great announcement.

Laying her hand on his arm, Delphine stole a look at Gascoigne and chided, 'Stop smiling! You are supposed to look miserable and trapped.'

'Sorry. I can't seem to stop.' His dimpled smile caused some young ladies to swoon as they moved through the crowd towards the family.

'Oh dear then, *I* will have to seem miserable for the announcement. We must give them something to talk about after all.' They exchanged such a complicit look that anyone who saw it had no doubt of the outcome of the sporting attraction.

The viscount looked at her in a way that caused a frisson of fear to course through Delphine's body.

It had been after all, a dangerous arrangement.

EPILOGUE

Miss Phoebe was packing her box, whilst Delphine was walking behind her, talking.

'You must stop, my dear Phoebe, I really cannot allow you to go.'

'We have had this out, my dear. Of course I will stay for the marriage, but after that I really must get back to Oakham. Although where I will put all my new finery,' she said, looking at the brown silk she was holding, 'is beyond-'

'You know my love that Gascoigne House must be renovated - I shall need your advice.'

Miss Phoebe smiled and turned to Delphine, 'And I, who have lived in a leaky cottage for ten years am the consultant you choose! My dear, you do not need me.' And she moved along, folding a petticoat carefully. 'I have told you before, young people need their privacy.'

'There are sixty rooms in Gascoigne Manor, I doubt that privacy is an issue. We shall probably have trouble finding each other.'

Her companion gave a thin smile at this sally, then continued her packing determinedly.

'Linen!' Said Delphine, inspired. 'You are wonderful with linen - and just think how much untended linen there must be at Gascoigne Manor - acres and acres, I expect.'

'I could-' started Miss Phoebe, and then 'no - it is absurd to invite me to live with you. You have done too much alr-'

'My fiancé is addicted to sporting pursuits!'

'Whatever-?'

'He is often out for hours. Sometimes away for days. And who will I talk to then?'

'Now, Delphine - I know you are being kind-'

'No indeed!' she grasped Miss Phoebe's hand and sat her down saying seriously 'I was so alone in Delacroix House. You can have no notion. Please Phoebe - do not leave me so again.'

Miss Phoebe threw herself in her friend's arms and wept. 'My dear girl,' she said, muffled against Delphine's shoulder. 'If you are really sure!'

Delphine patted her back, smiling.

#

That evening, the terminal meeting was held of *The Wed or Dead League*.

'Gentlemen,' toasted the viscount, 'we have all - except one - of us escaped this foully conceived League with our honour (just) and a new life. Let us bury its bones and seal the tomb and erstwhile meet only as friends.'

'Our secret to the grave gentlemen!' toasted the Marquis.

'To the grave!' Came the toast.

Author's Note:

Dearest Readers,

It's been a joy to me that my previous two Regency novels have been received so well and I do hope you have enjoyed Delphine's adventure. If you have, it would be kind of you to help others find it by ***leaving a review on Amazon.***

I'm also reminding you that you can get my short novella, Angelique and the Pursuit of Destiny, completely ***FREE here:*** *http://bit.ly/2vXZLhh . It isn't full length, but I think it maybe my favourite story of all!*

I'd like to thank a lot of people; all of my launch team and the myriad people who get a book published. Most especially ***Margaret Bandy*** *and* ***Denny Li*** *who were such fantastic beta readers.*

You can keep up to date and follow me on Twitter: ***@aliciaclarissa2*** *or on Facebook: https://www.facebook.com/aliciacameron.100/*

I genuinely love to hear from my readers, and you can contact me at: alicia@aliciacameron.co.uk.

Happy reading,
Alicia

Also available:

In paperback, eBook, and audiobook:

And also in eBook and audiobook, the Edwardian tales, a short story and a novella about a character who is unforgettable:

GetBook.at/Francine

GetBook.at/MissPhil

23958669R00134

Printed in Poland
by Amazon Fulfillment
Poland Sp. z o.o., Wrocław